THE ENEMY ABOVE

THE ENEMY ABOVE

MICHAEL P. SPRADLIN

SCHOLASTIC PRESS / NEW YORK

All rights reserved. Published by Scholastic Press, an imprint of Scholastic Inc., *Publishers since 1920*. SCHOLASTIC, SCHOLASTIC PRESS, and associated logos are trademarks and/or registered trademarks of Scholastic Inc.

Library of Congress Cataloging-in-Publication Data

Spradlin, Michael P., author.
  The enemy above / by Michael P. Spradlin.
    pages cm
  Summary: In 1942 twelve-year-old Anton, his family, and their small community of Ukrainian Jews are hiding from the advancing Nazis troops, and from the gestapo, in a web of underground caves, and one officer in particular, Major Karl Von Duesen, is determined to catch or kill every Jew he can find—but as the tide of war turns, a final confrontation between Anton and his enemy is looming.
  ISBN 978-0-545-85782-6
  1. Holocaust, Jewish (1939–1945)—Juvenile fiction.   2. Jews—Ukraine—History—20th century—Juvenile fiction.   3. Germany. Geheime Staatspolizei—Officers—Juvenile fiction.   4. World War, 1939–1945—Ukraine—Juvenile fiction.   5. Enemies—Juvenile fiction.   6. Fear—Juvenile fiction.   7. War stories.   8. Ukraine—History—20th century—Juvenile fiction.   [1. Holocaust, Jewish, (1939–1945)—Ukraine—Fiction.   2. Jews—Ukraine—Fiction.   3. Nazis—Fiction. 4. World War, 1939–1945—Ukraine—Fiction.   5. Ukraine—History—German occupation, 1941–1944—Fiction.]   I. Title.
  PZ7.S7645En 2016
  813.54—dc23
  [Fic]

                                                                      2015031408

10 9 8 7 6 5 4 3 2 1   16 17 18 19 20

Printed in the U.S.A.   23
First edition, July 2016

Book design by Christopher Stengel

In loving memory of my father, Hearl Spradlin,
born March 20, 1925, died August 13, 1989,
sergeant in the United States Army, 1943–1946.
He did his duty. I love you Dad.

I decided to devote my life to telling the story because I felt that having survived I owe something to the dead. And anyone who does not remember betrays them again.

—Elie Wiesel

At first, Anton thought the rumble was a summer storm. They often blew in from the west this time of year. The rain would sweep across the wheat fields, the far-off thunder sounding like an apple rolling across the wooden floor of his family's small farmhouse.

Yet when he looked up from the book he was reading and glanced through the window at the sky, no looming storm clouds marred the pink haze of twilight. The rumble was something else. In the distance, he saw flashes of light on the horizon. It wasn't lightning, nor fire. It was an explosion of artillery.

He stood and padded to the bedroom window as the noise grew louder. Shell after shell detonated and the night sky became a solid bank of light. Something truly horrible must be happening.

Anton watched the blasts for a moment longer. Battles always made him think of his father. Was he even still alive? It was 1942, and Papa had left their village in Ukraine to join the Polish army three years earlier, right before Hitler had begun his blitzkrieg across Eastern Europe. Poland, with its cavalry still riding horses, was little match for tanks and cannons. But Anton's father had joined the fight anyway. He'd said fighting Hitler was the only way to stop the madman.

"Are you out there, Papa?" Anton whispered. Then he prayed, asking God to please send his father home. And Uncle Pavel as well.

Pavel was nineteen years old. He was more a brother to Anton than to Papa. Every night at dinner, he'd talked of leaving the farm to join up with one of the partisan militias who were fighting the Nazis. But Anton's grandmother had always forbidden it.

"You will not go!" Bubbe would say. *Bubbe* was the Yiddish word for *grandmother*. She was old and her back was bent from years of hard work. Bubbe used a polished wooden walking stick, and when she spoke she would grab it from where it leaned against their dinner table and rap it firmly on the floor two times to emphasize a point. *Thump. Thump.* Everyone who knew Bubbe knew that when she thumped the walking stick, she was serious. It meant "pay attention." You were about to get a lecture.

"You will not leave your family. I have already given my oldest son. Your brother is a soldier, a prisoner, or a corpse. We have had no word from him since he left us. Your partisans are fools if they think they can stand against the Nazis. They are not trained or disciplined like a real army. And their ranks are riddled with spies. Those resistance fighters are just as likely to get you killed as if you joined the Russian army. I cannot lose you, too."

Pavel would keep his head down, shoveling potatoes and bread into his mouth. That was all they had to eat anymore. Oftentimes, there wasn't even any bread.

"Mother," he would say between bites. "I will not sit by and watch while Nazi dogs kill and enslave our people. What life do we have here? Every day they creep closer to us. They have been beaten back in Stalingrad, but soon they will be back and they will take everything. Everything! We cannot sit by and let them. We must fight."

"Fight." Bubbe would spit the word. "You are too young to know anything, Pavel. There is always someone fighting. Always someone taking. Our family has lived in the village of Borshchiv for centuries and always there is war. Someone hating and killing someone else. The Austrians, the Russians, the Polish, they fight endlessly over Ukraine. I will not lose another son to it. No more. You will not go."

Usually, Pavel would get up and storm off to the barn or go to the village square to listen to the gossip. Sometimes, he'd get his hands on a newspaper that was passed from household to household and scoured for information about the war. No one knew what to believe. The Germans were winning. The Russians were pushing them back. The English and Americans had landed in France, but the Germans pushed them back into the sea. No, the English and Americans had gained a foothold and were driving the Germans back. Hitler was fighting a war on two fronts and losing both. Still others said the English and Americans had not even landed in Europe, that they were concentrating on fighting in the South Pacific. No one knew the truth or what to believe.

"There is only one thing that is certain," Pavel would often say. "The Nazis are coming here. Hitler wants our fields and farms to feed his massive army. Whether they are winning or losing or the whole war is a stalemate, it does not matter. They are coming. But no one is coming to save us, Mother. We must save ourselves."

"Bah," Bubbe would say and throw up her gnarled hands. That signaled the end of any discussion.

Another of Anton's uncles, Dmitri, remained quiet whenever Pavel and Bubbe argued. He was the middle son. Anton sometimes thought things were hardest on Dmitri, caught in between his mother and younger brother. He'd worked harder to keep the family fed and clothed since Anton's father had left. And Anton knew Dmitri worried all the time. That Pavel would leave. That there wouldn't be enough food. That some night the door would be kicked in and their small house invaded by the gestapo.

Anton's bubbe and his uncles had tried to keep the stories from him, but he had heard them nonetheless. The Nazis and their leader, Adolf Hitler, hated Jews. At first, no one had believed the Nazis would be bold enough to do anything about it. But now they'd all heard too many tales of entire Jewish neighborhoods in cities to the west being rounded up and sent away. All over Europe, Jews fled their homes. But many waited, refusing to believe it could happen to them. Then the Nazis arrived. They blasted their way across the continent to prove the dominance of the Third Reich. And everywhere they went, Jews were rounded up, put on trains, and never seen again.

Now it seemed the fighting was upon them. The detonations grew louder. Flickering flames lit up the entire horizon. That could mean only one thing.

The Nazis were now destroying villages and towns on their way through Ukraine. If the Jews fled before they arrived, the Nazis would burn everything, making sure there would be nothing left for them to return to.

A loud explosion drew Anton's attention. It came from the northwest, toward the village.

The door to his room burst open. His grandmother stood in the doorway holding an oil lamp. The wick was turned down very low, giving off only the barest amount of light.

"Bubbe," Anton said. "They are getting closer. That explosion was only a few kilometers away."

"Yes, *kinder*. It is no longer safe here. I hoped this day would never come. But it is here. It is time for all of us to leave. We will meet the others at the crossroads. We must hurry and stay to the shadows. If we become separated, meet at Verbata. You know the way. Make sure you are not seen or followed. Trust no one. *No one*, kinder. The Nazis are offering rewards and extra rations for those who turn Jews in to the gestapo. Our home is now *Judenfrei*. We must careful."

Judenfrei was the German word meaning *free of Jews*. Anton had heard the village elders talk of the German army. They swept into towns and villages and either killed all the Jews immediately, or sent them off to the camps. Where once hundreds if not thousands of Jews might have lived, the gestapo made sure none remained. The gestapo was the Nazi secret police and they were tasked with finding and eliminating the Jews wherever they went.

Anton could not imagine it.

Bubbe thumped her walking stick twice on the floor. "Anton," she said, drawing him out of his morbid thoughts. "We must hurry. Gather up your things. Your uncles are coming. We will leave for the forest."

"But, Bubbe . . ." Anton said, before his words trailed off.

"What is it, my kinder?" No matter how big he got, Anton would always be a child to Bubbe.

"Nothing," Anton said. He hurried about his small room gathering up his meager belongings. He had been about to ask after his father. What if Papa came home and found them gone? How would he know where to find them? But Anton had noticed lately that whenever the subject of his father came up, Bubbe's eyes would water and her voice became a whisper. So he kept his questions to himself. Someday, when the war was over, his father would come back. Or Anton would go find him.

Oh, Papa, he thought. *How I miss you every day!*

Anton remembered how much his papa had loved to play pranks on his younger brothers. When they were working in the fields, Papa would stuff dirt down Pavel's pants and laugh as his hot-tempered little brother chased after him. When they still had horses, Papa would fiddle with the harnesses when Dmitri was plowing the fields. After a few rows the harness would become hopelessly tangled. Uncle Dmitri would curse and Papa's booming laugh could be heard all across the farm.

It seemed so long ago. Anton picked up the small photo of his father he kept on the table by his bedside. His mother had died of a fever when he was a baby. All he could remember of his childhood was his father and their life on the farm. Lately, when he was working in the fields or doing chores, he thought of his father. Of his rough hands. His deep laugh. His warm smile. But with every passing year, it was becoming more difficult to remember Papa's face. At night he would stare at the photo, determined to memorize each feature, from his father's rich black hair, to the dancing merriment in his eyes. But it seldom worked. Each day he felt Papa slipping further and further away.

The flickering light of the artillery lit up Anton's room as he gathered up his few possessions. Bubbe had prepared the family for the day the Nazis might come. He spread his warm woolen blanket out on the floor. On it he placed a pocketknife, a small hatchet, a tin cup, two changes of clothes, a few candles, and some matches. He rolled the blanket lengthwise until it formed a tube with his supplies in the middle. Then he folded it in half and tied the ends with cord. Now he could easily carry everything over his shoulder.

"Hurry, kinder," Bubbe shouted from the other room. "We must go."

Anton left his small room off the kitchen and joined his waiting grandmother. She stood by the door in a dark dress with a cloth scarf over her head, holding a cloth bag in one hand and her walking stick in the other.

"We will meet your uncles and the rest of our Jewish neighbors at the crossroads."

As they left their small home, it did not occur to Anton that he might never see it again. He had heard the elders talk about Borshchiv's history. It was surrounded by endless fields of wheat and potatoes and had been alternately claimed by Poland, Austria, and Russia in the last fifty years.

And now the Germans were coming. They might be the worst of all.

The noise from the artillery fire was growing louder. But the Russian army was far to the east. Who were the Nazis fighting? Perhaps members of the partisan militia or the Polish resistance? All the gossip said the Polish army had been crushed by the Germans' first attacks, but perhaps some of the fighters had survived? It seemed unlikely. But if Papa was among them, Anton would try to hold out hope.

"Bubbe," Anton said. "The fighting grows closer."

They quickened their pace. Anton took the cloth bag Bubbe carried so she could walk faster. He could not imagine being captured and sent to the camps. The degradation, the unsanitary conditions, the forced labor. Bubbe would never survive.

They traversed the wheat and potato fields surrounding their farmhouse and after walking several hundred meters they reached the tree line. Anton felt better. The night was cloudy and moonless, but he had felt exposed crossing the field. The Germans would have many vehicles patrolling the countryside and the gestapo was famous for using dogs to track down their victims. Among the trees they would at least be harder to spot.

About an hour later, they had almost reached the crossroads. Anton always thought it was funny to call the dirt paths that ran through their countryside *roads*. They hardly qualified. In the spring when the rains came, they turned into a muddy morass that oxcarts and livestock became hopelessly mired in. Yet they were the only way that the locals could travel or take their crops to market. Every farming family knew the countryside well. Perhaps that would keep them alive.

But they would have to hurry into hiding. Bubbe wasn't nimble enough to run for it if the Germans stumbled upon them. Anton was not sure how old she was. She never mentioned her age and had forbidden anyone from speaking of it. "I have been around a long time," she would say, "but I am wiser and smarter than all of you." His grandmother had worked hard all her life. Now her body was bent and she moved slowly, partly because her bones ached and partly because of the darkness. They finally reached the crossing and found a shadowed spot to wait for Anton's uncles. Anton helped Bubbe squat low in the wheat where they could be ready to hide should a German patrol pass by.

"Bubbe," Anton whispered. "Are you feeling ill?"

"No Anton, just old. I am not as spry as I used to be."

Anton made no mention of the fact that she called him by his name instead of "my kinder." Usually, that meant she was feeling serious, or that he was in trouble for shirking his chores. But tonight he knew it was because danger was near.

Anton looked to the west, where the sky still flashed with flickering light. Surely, it was too bright to have come only from exploding artillery shells. The Germans must have lit fires to burn nearby villages and farms. And now the destruction was creeping ever closer. Anton pictured a tiger, stalking them through the fields and forest. He imagined it might pop out and devour them at any moment.

They could do nothing but wait, and they did so in silence. According to Bubbe, Uncle Dmitri and Uncle Pavel would meet them here and lead them to a shelter they had found near the village of Verbata. Anton hoped they would arrive soon. Verbata was a friendly village, full of Jews and gentiles who knew each other well, and the thought of it made Anton feel safe.

A flash of light to the west drew his eye. This one was close. Too close. And it was not accompanied by an explosive blast. Instead, an engine revved, cutting through the quiet night.

"Anton, hide! Quickly," Bubbe urged. "They are here. The Germans are here."

Major Karl Von Duesen stood in the back of the half-track, scanning the horizon with his binoculars. The darkness and the vehicle's rough, jostling ride made it difficult to see anything. If he spotted any type of movement he would order the driver to stop. Then he could focus the lenses on whatever was running.

That is what the Jews were doing. Running. And those who had chosen not to run? Those who thought they could stand against the might of the Third Reich? They were no longer a problem. Major Von Duesen smiled. It had been a glorious day. His mission had been so successful he wondered if he might be given another promotion. If so, he would become the youngest lieutenant colonel in the gestapo.

As the terrain grew more uneven, the half-track's front tires rolled over every stone and its back treads bounced across every bump. Von Duesen dropped the binoculars and let them hang around his neck. He had volunteered to take a small unit to do some reconnaissance. Many of the Jews in the area had waited until the last moment, believing the blitzkrieg would fail. That somehow the pitiful Polish resistance fighters could oppose or halt the greatest army in the world. Now they were running. And that made them careless. Easy to catch. Still, the Germans were vulnerable. The Russian army still sat far to the east, but partisan forces and militias ran wild through the countryside. The militias were dangerous. They were composed of reserve soldiers from the Russian army who were older or perhaps too sick to fight, but they had weapons and they were organized. The partisan fighters were less of a threat to German forces. They were mostly civilians who opposed the current Ukrainian government for cooperating with the Reich. A bunch of university students and poets. Self-described intellectuals who ran around the countryside pretending to be soldiers. Karl Von Duesen did not fear them. But he would remain vigilant. Even bookworms could stage an ambush.

The headlights of the half-track cut sharply through the gloom. It was a cloudy, moonless night. But they had passed an empty farmhouse a few kilometers back. It had belonged to Jews, but now it was deserted. And tellingly, the mezuzah was gone. A mezuzah was a small container that observant Jews attached to the doorpost of their homes, containing special verses from the Torah written on parchment. But at this house, the mezuzah had been removed. Von Duesen knew that meant the occupants did not intend to return anytime soon.

Yet the ashes in the fireplace had still been glowing and the woodstove was warm. Whoever lived in the house had fled only recently. Which meant that, more than likely, they were still nearby. And Major Von Duesen would find them.

Up ahead, two dirt roads crossed each other. A flash of movement in the wheat field near the intersection caught the major's eye. He tapped the driver on the shoulder.

"*Halten*," he said. The driver hit the brake.

"Engine," he commanded. The driver turned the vehicle off. When the motor sputtered to a stop, Von Duesen listened carefully. He heard nothing. So he waited.

There was no chirp of insects or call of night birds. Perhaps the noise of the half-track had scared them away. And if the rustling he'd seen wasn't coming from the animals, it could mean only one thing.

Someone was nearby.

"Arms," he said. His driver and the two other men he brought with him took up their rifles and exited the vehicle. Von Duesen removed the Luger pistol from the holster at his belt.

"Fan out." He and his sergeant, a man named Eberhardt, took the right side of the half-track and the driver and another private took the left. Slowly, they crept forward, stepping lightly and listening for anything that sounded out of place. Von Duesen's pulse quickened and he tried to slow his breathing. There was someone close by, he was sure of it.

"Forward," he whispered. The four of them moved slowly, trying to make as little noise as possible. He flicked on his flashlight. They walked along the road until they reached the place where he thought he'd seen something move.

"Here," he whispered. He shone his light on the wheat field and spotted several crushed stalks, bent as if someone had recently tread on them as they passed through.

"Form up," he said. The four men made a line along the road facing the field. With hand signals, Major Von Duesen motioned them forward. He kept the Luger pointed straight in front of him. They entered the field single file, the others switching on their flashlights. Von Duesen was sure someone was close by. He could feel it. He wished he had brought a dog with him. The dogs were exceptional at tracking runners.

Cautiously, the men inched forward. Von Duesen swept the ground ahead of him with his flashlight. He was not afraid of the Jews. They did not fight back. But if resistance or militia fighters were nearby, the Germans' lights could give them away.

"Watch the tree line," he ordered. "If you see anything moving, shoot."

He followed the tramped-down trail through the wheat field. Someone had definitely come through here. But by the time they had almost reached the tree line, they had yet to spot anyone cowering in the field. Perhaps the runners had rushed across the field earlier and were long gone.

No. He was sure someone was close by. He could sense their fear.

"If you are here," he called loudly, "you must show yourself. I promise you will not be harmed."

There was no reply.

"Spread out," he said quietly.

The men widened the gap between them. Von Duesen waved them forward and they crept along, listening for their prey. But they heard nothing.

Suddenly, Von Duesen thought he heard what sounded like a human gasping for breath up ahead. He held up his hand and his men stopped instantly. Were his ears playing tricks on him? No, he was certain he had heard something. A noise that did not belong in a wheat field in the middle of nowhere.

Slowly, he snuck forward, his pistol raised. He swept the gun back and forth in front of him. They were about twenty-five meters from the tree line. He carefully examined the ground, expecting to discover a group of terrified Jews huddled together, cowering in fear.

But he saw nothing.

Where had they gone?

The Germans were now at the tree line. He glanced

behind him. Had they missed these mystery Jews somehow? Unlikely. He turned his attention to the forest ahead and considered his options. There were many more places to hide in the woods. He should have brought along the dogs.

"*Mein* major?" Sergeant Eberhardt asked. He was waiting for orders.

Major Von Duesen holstered his Luger.

"We will return to camp. Tomorrow when we have the light on our side we will come back and pick up the trail," he said.

The four men returned to their half-track and turned it back toward the east. It zoomed away in the night.

CHAPTER
THREE

Silence was life.

Stillness was freedom.

Anton turned his head to the dirt, so light would not reflect off his face. He curled his body tightly and tried to control his breathing, certain he was going to be discovered.

As the sound of the half-track grew nearer, he and Bubbe had hurried toward the tree line. But his grandmother had slowed them down. Behind them, he could hear the engine stop and the men leave the vehicle. He heard orders barked in German.

"Bubbe," he whispered. "Cover yourself with dirt." The soil was damp from the recent rains. He dug his hands into the ground and smeared his face and hands with mud. He helped his grandmother cover hers and pulled her shawl up around her face.

"When the soldiers come, you must make yourself

as small as possible and keep your face turned to the ground," he said.

"Be brave, my kinder," she said. He watched his grandmother curl herself into a ball. Many years of hard work on the farm had made her stiff, and she grunted with the effort.

Anton lifted his head slightly and studied the four men. They were spreading out along the road and he heard automatic weapons being cocked. The noise of the guns carried across the field so loudly he felt as if the sound was cutting through him. When the gestapo entered the wheat field, he ducked down, burrowing into the ground as best he could.

I must not look, he thought to himself. *I must not look.* He repeated the words over and over in his mind.

Anton focused on the sound of the approaching men. Their boots whispered through the wheat stalks. He wondered if he and Bubbe had somehow been spotted. The approaching vehicle had caught them by surprise. Anton willed himself to total stillness, praying that he could make himself invisible. To Anton, the men's footsteps sounded louder than cannon fire and he was certain his heart would explode. The voice of one of the soldiers startled him so much he nearly cried out.

Bubbe spoke several languages. Because of the war, he had not been able to attend school. But Bubbe had been teaching his lessons, and for the past several months she had been instructing him in German. So far he could understand and write it better than he could speak it. He heard the man ordering him and Bubbe to show themselves. Telling them that they would not be harmed. Anton wondered how this could be true. Their guns said otherwise.

Silence was life.

Despite the cool night air, Anton was sweating. He could not believe the men did not hear his heart hammering in his chest. He tried to keep his breathing regular, but it was difficult because he was so afraid.

The men were moving again. They would be upon him in moments. Should he run? Should he take Bubbe by the arm and make a break for the trees? No. They would never make it. The soldiers would gun them down before they had taken more than a step.

The soldiers inched closer. One of them was only meters away. The man's steps sounded like thunder. Anton desperately wanted to look, but he did not dare.

Stillness was freedom.

Every muscle in Anton's body tensed as he readied for rough hands to grab him and jerk him to his feet. But the man passed him by. Anton could hear him moving toward the trees. The soldier had walked right between him and Bubbe—huddled a couple meters apart—and not seen either of them.

What should they do? Would the men enter the forest? If they did, should he and Bubbe try to escape? Instinct told him to remain still.

A few moments later he heard the soldiers talking among themselves. They spoke in hushed, hurried tones. He could not hear well enough to understand. But he could tell that a decision had been reached. He glanced up quickly to see the men turning back and heading in his direction once again. Surely, he and Bubbe would be discovered.

Closer they came. But this time they were not as cautious. They hurried through the field and returned to the half-track. Anton heard the engine start and the vehicle roar away in the night.

He and Bubbe waited a few more minutes, then stood up. Bubbe groaned with the effort. She picked her way across the field slowly, taking sharp breaths as her joints creaked. Anton wished she could move faster, in case the Nazis returned. He took her by the arm to steady her while she walked.

"You are a good boy, kinder," she said, patting him on the wrist.

"Thank you, Bubbe," he said. "We must hurry."

"They will not return tonight," she said.

"How do you know?"

"Because I am old and wise. But my hearing is still young." Bubbe cackled with laughter. "And my German is better than yours."

Anton had to smile. But as they made their way toward the shelter of the woods, Anton couldn't help looking over his shoulder.

CHAPTER
FOUR

Von Duesen had caught so many Jews in the last twenty-four hours his commanding officer, General Steuben, did not mind that his night reconnaissance had been a bust. Von Duesen stood ramrod straight in the general's quarters as he finished his debriefing. A large map of the area was pinned to the wall.

"Today we searched all around this area here." Von Duesen pointed out his route. "We found many abandoned farmhouses and took a total of thirty-six prisoners into custody."

"Excellent work, Major," the general said. Von Duesen nodded in appreciation.

"Once the area is *Judenfrei* and the country is ours, we will be able to relocate many of our people here. The farming is excellent, the soil quite fertile. This may become the fuel that drives the Reich to conquer all of Europe. The land here could grow enough crops to feed thousands—maybe millions." General Steuben grew excited at the thought. The gestapo knew the führer's master plan. Once this area was cleared of Jews and the Russian army was defeated, Hitler would relocate German citizens here to farm and expand the empire.

"*Ja*," the general went on. "Ukraine is indeed rich in resources. When the Russian army is crushed, we will control an entire continent. Our enemies will fold like tents in the wind before the might of the Reich."

"Heil Hitler," Von Duesen said as he performed the traditional salute. But part of him doubted the boasting general. Karl's brother, Heinz, was serving with a German infantry battalion on the Russian front. In truth, the German army was retreating after vicious fighting in the city of Stalingrad. The Battle of Stalingrad had been a disaster. Heinrich had written him that though the Russians were outnumbered, outgunned, and without supplies, they simply refused to give up.

In the end, the Russians would not be broken. They called upon every able-bodied citizen, including children, women, and old men—anyone able to hold a rifle—and they fought like demons. They made the soldiers of the Reich pay in blood for every plot of soil they took. The German army was now regrouping in the east, while the Russians licked their wounds and prepared to go on the offensive. The führer was considering what to do. The word from London was that the Americans and British were not ready to attempt to retake Europe. They had overwhelmed the German army in North Africa and were on the move against vastly inferior Italian troops in Italy. But for now, the Reich held the bulk of Europe and had only the Russians to contend with. Millions of angry, bloodthirsty Russians who wanted revenge.

But Von Duesen was not yet ready to believe the Reich could be defeated. Their blitzkrieg tactics had earned them control over almost the entire European continent. Setbacks in Africa and Russia were nothing to worry about. Karl was a believer. He always had been. Born in Munich to a wealthy family, he had been a prominent leader in the Hitler Youth movement during his university days. When he graduated he had joined the army. Karl was smart, but more importantly he was cunning. And he had moved up quickly through the ranks. Now he was the youngest officer of his rank in the gestapo. His tall, strong body, cropped blond hair, and intense blue eyes made him a poster boy for the führer's master race. An Aryan nation that would rule the world.

No. He shook the negative thoughts from his head. The Reich would prevail. Of this he was certain. Adolf Hitler had restored the pride of the German people after the humiliating defeat of World War I. And when they conquered their enemies this time around, a glorious new day would dawn. He was glad to do his part.

"What are my orders, *mein* general?" he asked.

"The same, Major," he replied. "The same."

Von Duesen smiled. Tomorrow he would return to the field. And he would hunt.

Soon, all of Ukraine would be *Judenfrei*.

CHAPTER FIVE

"Where are we going, Bubbe?" Anton asked as they trekked through the dark woods toward Verbata. It was slow going. They picked their way carefully across the forest floor. Anton guided Bubbe over knobby roots and under low-hanging branches to make sure she did not fall.

"Your uncles have found a shelter for us," she said. "Dmitri says it's big enough to hide us and many other Jewish families. But he and Pavel have not told me where it is. They will find us and lead us there. If the gestapo captures us before then, we cannot reveal the location if we do not know it."

Anton thought about that. It was a good plan. However, after the encounter with soldiers earlier he decided he would feel better if he knew where they were going. The forest hid them temporarily, but soon they would once again have to cross open ground.

"They were not at the crossroads," Anton said.

"I'm sure they saw the soldiers. Do not worry, kinder. They will find us."

"How do you know?"

"Because I have faith. God will provide." The way she said it told him the subject, as far as she was concerned, was closed.

Looking up at the stars that peeked through the clouds, Anton was fairly certain they were headed north. Finally, they emerged from the forest onto a dirt path through another wheat field. The going was easier now and they made better time.

Until Anton heard the snap of a branch up ahead and stopped in his tracks.

"Shh, Bubbe. Wait," Anton whispered. Taking her by the arm, he led her off the path and back into the wheat. *Snap!* Whatever was making that sound, it was getting closer. Anton spied a wagon pulled by a team of horses and driven by two men. All he could tell was that they were dressed in dark clothing. But he dared not call out. Collaborators were everywhere. Sometimes, they captured Jews and took them to the Germans, hoping for a reward. Other times they simply reported the Jews' whereabouts. Who was to say the men in the wagon were not dangerous?

"*Muter?*" one of the men whispered. *Mother.* Anton sighed in relief, recognizing his uncle Dmitri's voice. He and Bubbe stepped into the road as the wagon rolled to a stop.

"Uncle Dmitri!" Anton tried, and he could not keep the excitement out of his voice.

Dmitri smiled at his nephew. "We thought you might come this way when we saw the gestapo in the wheat field," he said. "This is Sergei, a baker from Verbata. He's lent us the use of his wagon. Come, now. We must hurry." The two older men helped lift Bubbe into the wagon seat. Dmitri drove the team, while Anton and Sergei settled into the back of the wagon, which was loaded with supplies. They sat atop a number of burlap sacks. Anton smelled potatoes and cabbage.

Bubbe stared at Dmitri and pursed her lips. "Where is Pavel?" she demanded.

Dmitri sighed. Anton could tell his uncle did not want to answer. But Bubbe would not be denied. "He's gone. To the militia. He knew you would not understand. But he loves you, *Muter*. He promises to come back to you."

Bubbe closed her eyes and did not speak a word. What was there to say? Pavel's fate was now in God's hands.

"Where are we going, Uncle Dmitri?" Anton asked.

"Someplace safe," Dmitri said.

"Is it far?" he pressed his uncle.

"It is as far as it needs to be, Anton," Dmitri said. "Many Jews have been taken. We cannot outrun the German army. So we will run as far as we can. Then we will hide."

Anton was about to ask another question, but his uncle interrupted him. "I understand you are nervous and afraid. But we must travel quietly. The noise of the wagon will drown out the approach of foot patrols. We must be silent and listen and watch. Pay attention to the sounds of the night birds. Study the horizon. If you see something, say something. I promise all of your questions will be answered soon."

Anton did as his uncle instructed. The four of them

traveled along the path in silence. The ground was rough and uneven, and the wagon squeaked and groaned as the horses plodded over the bumpy terrain.

With each passing moment, Anton grew more uneasy. The encounter with the soldiers in the wheat field had completely unnerved him. Up until now, the war, the Nazis, and their *Judenfrei* policy had all seemed like some distant, abstract thing. Just gossip that the elders in the village square used to add drama to their stories. Newspapers used the rumors to frighten people and sell more papers.

But tonight he had seen the soldiers walk past him, close enough to touch. Soldiers with guns who would shoot him down if they spotted him. Everything he had heard was true. He was just a twelve-year-old boy and yet they hunted him. He had broken no laws, done nothing wrong. He was simply born Jewish. How could anyone want to kill him for it?

As the wagon rolled on, he could not help but imagine that there were Nazis watching him now. Perhaps they hid in the shadows, following the wagon until it arrived at their hiding spot. Once there, the gestapo would burst from their hiding places and capture Anton's family and the others who were only looking for a safe place to hide.

Bubbe had told stories of the pogroms, tales of how the old Russian czar had sent Cossacks—his soldiers—into Jewish villages all over Ukraine. Thousands of Jews were dragged from their homes and shops. The lucky ones were only forced to watch their homes and businesses burned to the ground. The unlucky ones were murdered. His other grandmother, Ruth, had been unlucky. Those who could fled in fear. Now they were running again. And this time they were being hunted. Bubbe would often tell Anton that she hoped a day would come when he might live as a Jew without fear. That day seemed a long way off.

Anton tried to do as his uncle instructed. He strained to listen to the sounds of the night. He scanned the horizon for suspicious movement. The fact that it was a moonless night was a blessing and a curse. The lack of light kept them hidden, but it cloaked their enemies as well. The farther they traveled, the more ragged and nervous his breath grew. Sweat crawled across his forehead and trickled down his cheeks, disappearing beneath the collar of his shirt.

Several times he thought he saw something odd and nearly called out in alarm. But each time, the mysterious lurker proved to be only a tree or bush, not a waiting Nazi. Whenever it happened, Anton felt foolish. But he forced himself to remain vigilant.

Finally, Uncle Dmitri pulled the reins and the wagon came to a stop.

"We're here."

Anton was confused. They were in an open meadow, with only a small copse of trees and a pile of boulders nearby. There were no buildings, no cabins, not even a tent. Could his uncle be lost?

"I do not understand. Is this it? Are we going to build our shelter?" Anton asked.

"Yes, Anton, this is it. But our shelter is already built," Dmitri said.

"But there is nothing here," Anton said.

"You will see. You and Bubbe will remain here with the supplies, while Sergei and I gather more food," Dmitri said, helping Bubbe down from the wagon seat.

"But we will not be safe out here in the open," Anton insisted.

"Patience, Anton," Dmitri said. "Follow me."

Sergei remained with the wagon. Dmitri took Bubbe by the arm, leading her toward the rock formation, which stood about forty meters off the road.

Anton followed along, carefully picking his steps in the darkness. He could not imagine how his uncle could consider this a safe place.

Then they arrived at the boulders and he understood. Two of the giant rocks tipped against each other. There was a small space between them. It was the opening to a cave.

Dmitri led them inside. They had to descend a small slope, but eventually the floor leveled out. Once safely inside, a match was struck and an oil lamp lit, illuminating the faces of at least twenty people. All of them had come for the same reason. Their cheeks were streaked with dirt. Their eyes were tired, their expressions laced with worry.

But for the moment they were safe.

Anton studied the group in the flickering light of the lamp. He knew many of them, but there were faces he'd never seen. He counted twenty-eight in the band. Six of them were men about his uncle's age. The rest were women and children. And off to the side of the group, Anton noticed one solitary boy who looked about his age.

Dmitri motioned to the men to help him empty the wagon of supplies.

Bubbe stood before the rest of the group, leaning on her walking stick. She studied their tired faces. Anton knew she was exhausted. But she straightened herself and thumped her walking stick on the floor of the cave two times. Anton could not help but smile.

"Some of you I recognize," she began. "You, Rina, your father was Levi Rosen?" The woman nodded and smiled. "You were a teenager the last time I saw you.

We will all be getting well acquainted with one another soon enough. I know you are tired and scared. But we will conquer our fear. For the time being, we are safe. We have shelter, food, and each other. All of you have left your homes, your communities. We will make a new community here. God will watch over us. With his guidance all of us have made our way here on this night. What we have, we share. We will care for the children, take turns cooking, and turn this cave into a home. The men will go out looking for food each evening. We can only hope the darkness will keep them hidden. When they return in the daytime, we will stand watch so they can rest.

"There is one more thing we must all remember. If we are discovered, we are to gather north of here, near Verbata. There is another underground place called the Priest's Grotto. It isn't close and the journey would be dangerous. But the countryside is full of farmers who will help us. Do not forget the Priest's Grotto. It will not be easy. But when have our lives ever been easy?"

She paused and looked at each face in turn. "United, we are stronger than we are alone. Now, let us all work together so we may get settled in and make our shelter more inviting. But first let us all introduce ourselves to one another. I am Erica Schostak. This handsome boy is my grandson, Anton." She raised her walking stick and pointed it at Anton. His face flushed red. The women chuckled. And one by one they said their names. Rosen. Grossman. Weiss. Birnbaum. Serniov. Fetisov. By then, two of the children had fallen asleep on a pile of blankets. With the introductions done, everyone sprang to work. Rina took Bubbe by the arm, led her to a small stool, and helped her sit. She left Bubbe there a moment before returning with a cup of water.

Anton took a moment to study the cave. The oil lamps they'd brought made shadows dance and flicker across the cavern floor. The limestone walls were dark and grooved in places where water had seeped through the ground. Anton thought it must have taken centuries for the water to erode the rock. But the cave was warm and reasonably dry, even if it smelled like wet dirt.

He felt Bubbe's hand on his shoulder. She had left her seat. "Anton," she said. "This is Daniel. His father is in the army, like yours."

"Hello," Anton said.

"Hello," Daniel replied.

Bubbe motioned to Dmitri and the other men who had returned with the rest of the wagon's supplies. "I am sure the two of you can help make the cave more comfortable. Anton, why don't you introduce Daniel to your uncle?" Bubbe said. She used the tone of voice he had heard many times before. It meant that he had no choice in the matter.

Anton smiled at Daniel. "I guess we're going to be friends."

Daniel nodded his head nervously. He didn't say much as Anton led him to Uncle Dmitri. And true to Bubbe's word, they were both given a list of chores.

Anton looked around their new home with apprehension. The entrance to the cave may have been a narrow tunnel, but once through it, the main chamber was large and open with little nooks where a person might find some solitude. Toward the back of the cavern, tunnels led off in many directions. The cave was dark. And the light of the oil lamps was swallowed up quickly. The farther back they ventured, the stronger the smell of wet dirt became. Anton supposed they would get used to it. As he'd noticed earlier, the walls of the cave were damp, but he did not hear the sound of a stream or river. What would they do for water, he wondered? He supposed they would need to carry it in from the outside.

"Do not venture too far down the passageways or tunnels," Uncle Dmitri warned them. "These caves go on for many kilometers with dozens of twists and turns. It would be easy to become hopelessly lost. But should we be discovered, this maze will work to our advantage. If the gestapo, the SS, or the Ukrainian secret police ambush us, you must scatter and hide. Hurry down the tunnels as far as you can. The darkness will be your friend. Discovery is unlikely—we are well hidden here. But it is best to be prepared."

Suitably warned, Anton and Daniel went to work. They stacked burlap bags of vegetables and baskets of bread. Then they grabbed several bales of hay and helped the younger girls finish making straw mattresses for everyone.

"Can you show me how to do this?" Daniel asked a small girl with dark hair and big eyes. "Your mattresses look much more comfortable than mine.

Whoever gets this one isn't going to sleep very well, I'm afraid."

The little girl, Lena, giggled. "Like this," she demonstrated.

Daniel was good with the children, Anton observed. He had them joking and laughing and soon they were making a game out of their work. Racing to see who could make the most mattresses. Anton soon realized the girls were all developing crushes on Daniel. Anton was somewhat awestruck. He was far too shy around girls, even young ones.

As he worked, Anton began to realize that people had been toiling in the cave for quite a while. Someone must have known about this place and set it up as the perfect rendezvous point if the Germans arrived. Larger alcoves dug and chiseled out by hand dotted the walls so that families could have their own space. A central kitchen area had been built near the back of the main cavern. Someone had even brought a small stove. Several of the women were peeling vegetables and tending to a simmering stew. For a moment, Anton allowed himself to relax. Perhaps this place would be safe.

Once the supplies were stored and the spaces

divided up, Dmitri called everyone to gather around a single oil lamp.

"We have made a good start today," he said. "However, this is not a perfect place for us. We do not have fresh water. Which means Sergei, Leonid, Slava, Herman, Yakov, and I will likely need to make several trips out per night in order to bring back enough for all of us. The rest of you will stay behind. Daniel and Anton, it will be your job to keep watch for German patrols. We must not light a fire or the lamps often, only to cook and only in the daytime. Does everyone understand?"

Anton was disappointed. True, he was scared of being captured. But he wanted to go out at night and forage for supplies. He wanted to help, not stay behind as a glorified lookout. He would wait until the time was right and talk to his uncle. He knew where to find food. Even though most of the harvest was done, there were orchards where you could still find fruit. The surrounding fields held shocks of wheat that could be gathered up and ground into flour. He could be useful. That was what he wanted. To make a difference.

The meeting was over. Parents gathered their children and shuffled off to their own small spaces. But Anton noticed that Daniel stood by the lamp, shifting back and forth on his feet.

"Are you alone here?" Anton asked him.

Daniel stared at the ground. "Yes." He didn't elaborate, and Anton didn't press him. Everyone deserved a few secrets. The boy's face was gaunt and he had dark shadows under his eyes. Clearly, he had not been sleeping or eating regularly for some time. Anton knew there were things that were difficult to put into words. And sometimes, talking only made a person remember what was best forgotten. Daniel would talk when he was ready.

"If you like, there is a space back there big enough for two. We can each drag one of the mattresses back there," he offered.

"What about your grandmother? Shouldn't you stay with her?" Daniel asked tentatively.

Anton shrugged. "She snores. Come on. If we're going to keep watch during the night, we're going to need to be rested."

Anton led Daniel to an alcove that was barely wide enough for their two straw mattresses. As they arranged their sleeping quarters, Anton told Daniel about his uncle Pavel and how much he was worried about him. "With my father gone, it is difficult for the family to be separated even further."

Daniel was quiet for a moment. "I know exactly what you mean," he said. "My mother—"

Anton noticed Daniel's jaw clenching tightly. "You don't have to tell me anything," he said.

But now that he'd started talking, Daniel wouldn't be stopped. "My village is just a small place north of Borta. It is hardly a village at all, really. It has a store and a synagogue and a few houses clustered around a cross-roads. Not much ever happens there. We farm and worship and live quiet lives. Then the Nazis arrived and our quiet lives were suddenly very noisy. No one knows why they attacked. Usually, they entered a town or village and simply took over. We were peasants. Farmers. We could offer them no resistance.

"Yet they came in with tanks and half-tracks shooting down people in the street. Jews, gentiles, it did not matter. They were filled with bloodlust. Soldiers went from house to house dragging my neighbors outside into the street and gunning them down. Our farmhouse was on the outskirts of the village. My mother and sister and I tried to get away. But my sister was too small to run. I could not carry her. My mother tried, but she was not fast enough. The Nazis caught them. My mother screamed at me to run and hide . . . and I did. I ran to the fields. I left them. Later, I saw them loaded onto a truck and taken away. I don't know where. I stumbled upon Sergei and his wagon and he told me about this place."

Daniel clenched his fists. "I should have fought those monsters. If I were stronger, my family would still be together."

Anton could see moistness in Daniel's eyes. He did not know what to say. Only that without hope, Daniel would never survive this awful war.

"I am so sorry. I cannot imagine witnessing such a thing. But think of it. As far as you know your mother and sister are still alive. My bubbe is always telling me that God will provide and watch over us. And he will watch over your family, too . . ."

"Anton, I mean no disrespect to your bubbe. I'm sure you love her as much as I loved mine. And I mean no disrespect to you, either. But where was God when the Nazis attacked our village? Where was he when they took my mother and sister? Where was God when they shot Mr. and Mrs. Hagerbaumer? They were our village elders. They couldn't fight. Yet the Germans shot them down like dogs. Where was God then?"

Daniel's voice was full of anger. Anton did not know what to do. Nothing he could say would make a difference. Perhaps Daniel just needed time. He vowed to listen to him when he talked. Perhaps a friendly ear would help.

"I am sorry," Anton repeated. "I will pray that your family is safe."

"What will we do?" Daniel asked. It was a large and loaded question. How were they going to survive? Would they find Daniel's family? Was either of their fathers still alive? The war could not last forever. If they managed to outlast it, what would the rest of their lives look like if no one was around to help them pick up the pieces?

"I do not know, Daniel," Anton said. "Bubbe says . . ." No. This moment wasn't about his grandmother's wisdom, or even about his own need to believe that everything would be fine. This was about taking comfort where they could, and forcing themselves to carry on. "I think it is up to us. For now, I think we just try to make it through each day alive."

Daniel did not answer. Anton lay down on his mattress and in a matter of seconds sleep overtook him.

That night he did not dream.

CHAPTER
SEVEN

After the first few days in the cave, a sort of benign boredom set in. At night the men ventured out and returned several times with buckets of water, which were transferred to barrels in the cavern. During the day, a little sunlight crept into the cave's entrance, but Anton noticed that it didn't really penetrate the darkness or the gloom. Everyone tried to keep busy, but there wasn't much they could do without risking discovery. The children couldn't play loud games. The women cooked only during the day, so no passersby would notice the light of the stove.

Anton and Daniel kept watch each night. But they didn't see anything suspicious. Yet Anton knew the Germans had overrun the countryside. Patrols were everywhere, Dmitri said. He and Sergei had gone to the river to gather water and had nearly been caught twice. But Anton and Daniel never saw anyone anywhere near the entrance to the cave.

On the fourth day, Dmitri called them to his side.

"I have a mission for the two of you," he said.

Anton grew excited, but tried not to show it. "How may we help, Uncle?" he asked.

"Our nightly excursions are becoming more dangerous. Last night we were nearly captured yet again. A squad of gestapo followed us, but we lost them in the woods. We led them away from the cave, so it took us twice as long to return. We had to dump out the water we were carrying so we could travel faster."

He stared solemnly at each boy. "The danger is becoming too grave for us. So tonight while we are out, I want the two of you to explore the cave. Elsa and some of the other women will keep watch."

"What are we looking for?" Daniel asked.

"A good question, Daniel," Dmitri said, placing his hand on the boy's shoulder.

"Two things," Dmitri said. "The first is to find out if any of the cave's passageways lead to an underground spring. If we can find a water source in the cave, we will not have to venture out each night. Second, look for another way out of this cave. We need an escape hatch. If we are discovered—if the gestapo should come here—we must have a way to flee."

He handed a flashlight and a canteen to Anton, and a small bag of bread and fruit to Daniel.

"I thought you said the passageways were full of twists and turns. How will we keep from becoming lost?" Anton said.

Dmitri handed him a rock. It felt soft and chalky in his hand.

"Use the rock to mark your way. This limestone will leave a visible line on the rock, like chalk. Draw an arrow every fifty steps. If you become lost, you will follow them back to the main cavern. Any questions?"

Anton and Daniel shook their heads, understanding what was required of them.

"We'll go now," Anton said. "No time like the present."

"Good. Be careful. Don't take any unnecessary chances. Don't forget that this cave can be dangerous."

Anton flicked on the flashlight and Dmitri checked his pocket watch. "Go as far as you can in one hour, then turn back. If you do not return in two hours, someone will come looking for you." Dmitri placed the watch in Anton's hand and left them, returning to the group warming themselves by the stove.

"Shall we?" Anton said.

"I guess," Daniel said. "I do not like the dark. I would rather we were hiding in the treetops than in these underground caves."

Anton knew that Daniel was still worried about his mother and sister; he didn't want his new friend to have anything else to fret over. "It will be fine. We're safe here," Anton said.

"We are not safe anywhere," Daniel muttered as they entered one of the passageways. Anton had no answer for that.

A few meters down the path, the ceiling got lower and they had to hunch over to continue. But after about fifty meters the cave widened again and they could stand up straight. So far, the path had not split from the main tunnel, but every fifty steps they dutifully marked the walls, drawing an arrow pointing toward the main cavern.

Anton watched Daniel take cautious steps along

the path. It was almost as though Daniel thought that if they could just be silent enough, nothing bad could happen to them. He was nervous, and his breath came in ragged gasps. Anton wanted to help him relax but couldn't think of a way to do it.

After another seventy-five meters, they came to a fork in the passageway.

"Which way?" Anton asked. He shone the light down both paths but it revealed nothing of promise in either direction.

"Let's go to the right. But since we'll have to come back and explore the other direction anyway, it really makes no difference," Daniel said.

They headed to the right and followed the passage for several meters, marking their way and keeping track of the time. Twenty-five minutes had passed. As they walked farther down the tunnel, Anton observed that the cave was growing damper.

"Look," he said, rubbing his fingers over the slick rock walls. "Water. I wonder where it is coming from?"

"It could be water seeping in from the ground above," Daniel said.

"Perhaps," Anton said. But he was excited at the prospect. It might be a spring. Or perhaps they might find an underground creek.

Anton stopped at the driest spot he could find and marked the wall with an arrow. A few meters farther on, the passage narrowed and they had to walk single file. Then it narrowed further, so they had to turn sideways to move forward.

"Perhaps we should turn back," Daniel suggested. "I would much prefer it. Turning back would be good, I think."

Anton tried not to chuckle at Daniel's discomfort, but it was difficult. And with the walls as wet as they were, Anton thought giving up now would be a mistake. They could be close to a water source that would solve their problems! "Why don't I go just a little bit farther. If I don't find anything, we'll head back."

Daniel was about to agree when a noise stopped him in his tracks.

"Do you hear that?" Anton asked.

"What is it?"

"Water dripping, I think. It's coming from up ahead. I have to find out for sure."

"But the passage is too narrow," Daniel said.

"I think I can make it."

"I don't think this is a good idea, Anton."

"Don't worry. It will be fine. You wait here. Keep an eye on the watch. I will try to make it as far as I can. Call out to me in fifteen minutes. If I haven't found anything by then, I'll come back."

Anton knew Daniel did not approve, but he couldn't let that bother him now. They needed water to live. The ceiling was so low he needed to drop to his hands and knees. He began to crawl, and soon Daniel was out of sight.

As Anton scurried along, the sound of the water grew to a steady drip. Now both the walls and floor of the cave were covered in moisture. And the water had to be coming from somewhere. Anton pushed ahead, and as the passageway opened back up, he hopped back to his feet, which were soaked. The water was two or three centimeters deep.

Drip. Drip. Drip. Anton pointed the flashlight upward and saw where the water was coming from. His heart sank. The ceiling above him was a collection of small rocks and boulders held in place by mud and dirt. Water from the recent rains had worked its way in between the rocks and dripped into the cave from above. There was no spring here, no creek. Anton shone the light over the rocks, wondering if their group could collect enough water here to satisfy their needs. *Not a chance*, he thought. Even if they could manage to get their buckets through the narrow tunnel, they'd never fill them fast enough. It had been raining the past few days, and this runoff from the storms wouldn't last a day.

"Anton!" Daniel's shout startled him. Anton had forgotten all about the time. He could hear how anxious his friend was.

"It has been fifteen minutes! Are you all right?" Daniel's voice echoed off the cave walls.

"Yes, I'm fine," Anton said. "I'll be back with you in a moment."

But first, he had to do one more thing. Their mission was to find a water source. But they were also supposed to be looking for an exit. He reached up to one of the boulders above him and pushed. At first, nothing happened.

But then he heard the sound of rock sliding on

rock. The boulder came loose from the ceiling and nearly fell on top of him! With all his strength, Anton pushed it aside. But once one was dislodged, the others came crashing down. "Dan—"

He could not get the words out of his mouth before another large rock fell from the ceiling and slammed into his shoulder, driving him to his knees. And that was just the beginning. Rock after rock pelted every part of his body. He tried to shout in alarm, but the words caught in his throat. His flashlight was knocked from his hand and it skittered away, leaving him in darkness.

This was bad. Very bad. Uncle Dmitri would never trust him with responsibility again. The crush of that realization seemed more than Anton could bear. And then a rock the size of a melon grazed the side of his head.

He remembered nothing else.

CHAPTER
EIGHT

Major Von Duesen stood in the back of the half-track, his eyes roaming the countryside. It was nearing midnight and the waxing crescent moon gave off just enough light that they could run the vehicle without headlights. The engine did make some noise, but the darkness still gave them a small advantage over their quarry. Light traveled farther than sound. Those they hunted would not hear the engine until the Germans were too close for them to escape.

Von Duesen was frustrated. He knew there were Jews hiding in the area, but they had gone to ground. And they had hidden themselves well. For the last three nights he had returned from patrol empty-handed. But the Reich's extensive records showed that there were still a number of people unaccounted for.

At first, he was certain that sympathizers were hiding the remaining Jewish families. But he and his squad had searched dozens of farmhouses, shops, and even the homes of gentiles he suspected of defying the Reich by hiding Jews from the gestapo. Each time he had come up empty.

There had been rumors. He had heard whispers from his informants that a large group of Jews was hidden somewhere near the small village of Borta. Each night, he and his men would search the tiny hamlet, then work outward, circling like a shark around a reef. Yet they continually failed to find their prey.

Tonight he had taken a different approach. The day had begun the same as those before. His team searched the obvious hiding places: abandoned barns, a deserted church, farms owned by suspected sympathizers. But none of them were hiding Jews.

Karl had always assumed that fear of the gestapo would force the *Juden* to make mistakes. They might cower in their hiding places now, but soon they would crack. And his unit would be waiting to catch them. As the führer had taught his followers, Jews were feeble and slow-witted. Unworthy of standing in the shadow of the master race. Major Von Duesen would not allow the travesty of their evasion to continue. But where were they?

All day he had studied the map and surveillance photos of the surrounding area. The map was five years old, but it was the most recent one of the area they could find. It did not include some of the newer farms, but it marked all the roads and rivers. He had pored over it in recent days, memorizing every field, every pond. What was he missing?

"Water," he murmured. A thought had suddenly occurred to him.

"*Was, mein* major?" his sergeant asked.

Von Duesen did not answer immediately. He was thinking. If the Jews had been hidden by a gentile farmer, they'd have had access to a well. But anyone who didn't have that kind of help—anyone hiding out in the wilderness of the countryside—they would need to be near a lake, stream, or spring. These Jews might have been able to stash enough food to stay alive for weeks or months in their hiding place. But they could not live without water.

"*Halten*," he ordered. The private driving the half-track braked to a stop. Von Duesen pulled a map from his pocket. He jumped out, spread open the map on the hood of the vehicle, and switched on his flashlight. The three other men of his squad crowded around him.

He found the village of Borta. It was logical to assume that those in hiding would remain close to the village. Even if they had stores of food, they would eventually run out. The closer they were to places where they knew they might replenish their supplies, the less time they would have to be out in the open where they might be caught. They knew this area. Why flee to the unfamiliar?

Von Duesen's finger traced over the wrinkled paper. North of the village was a small stream. It was isolated. There were some open fields and farmlands around it, but the stream itself ran through a wooded area that would provide good cover. There were no houses close by, and so it was unlikely that anyone creeping along that part of the stream would be spotted. The Jews must be hiding somewhere within walking distance of this place!

"Beeilen Sie sich!" he said to his men. *Hurry.*

They scrambled back into the half-track and turned it around. Von Duesen's driver went as fast as he dared with the headlights off. The vehicle bounced over the rough terrain. If they were not careful they could overturn. But in Von Duesen's mind there was no time to waste. When they emerged from the fields and turned onto a dirt road, the major finally exhaled.

A half hour later, they had reached their destination. Von Duesen ordered his men to take up their weapons.

"Schnell! Schnell!" he hissed. *Fast. We must be fast*, he thought. He was sure he would find what he was looking for here. His men grabbed their machine guns and followed him toward the trees at a brisk trot. Von Duesen's eyes scanned the horizon.

"*Halten Sie*," he whispered, holding his hand up in a fist. *Hold*.

He'd seen something move in the trees ahead. Two men scurried through them carrying large milk cans mounted on a wooden staff between them. Their silhouettes were barely visible, but the longer he watched, the more sure he became. He had found the Jews he was looking for.

Now Major Von Duesen had a decision to make. Should he take these men prisoner and interrogate them until they revealed where the others were concealed? Or should he follow them? If he tracked them back to their hiding place, he might capture the entire group. He had only a moment to decide before he lost the men in the darkness. Capturing a large number of Jews would surely win him favor with General Steuben. A medal for certain. Perhaps even a promotion. He could become the youngest lieutenant colonel in the gestapo.

He motioned for his squad to follow and they quietly shadowed the two men. For now, he would trail them. It was the easier of the two options. But if they noticed, he would capture them, question them, and break them. They would reveal the location of their camp. He smiled in the darkness.

No matter what happened, Major Karl Von Duesen of the gestapo would not return to headquarters tonight empty-handed.

CHAPTER NINE

"Anton! Anton!" He heard his name shouted from a far-off place. He wanted to open his eyes but could not. Something was wrong with them. He felt as if an enormous weight was pressing down on his eyelids. And even when he managed to pry them open, his world was still shrouded in darkness.

"Anton!" the voice cried out again.

Slowly, his memory returned. The voice belonged to Daniel. Uncle Dmitri had sent them to explore the cave's tunnels. And he had thought he might have found a back way out of the cave. And then the rocks fell. Though his head ached, he was glad he could remember what had happened. It must mean he was not terribly injured.

"Anton!" Daniel called again.

Anton tried to answer but his voice was an awkward croak. His mouth and throat were clogged with dust. When he coughed, pain shot through his ribs and head. The weight of the fallen rocks pressed down on top of him, holding him immobile.

"I'm here," he moaned.

"Are you injured?"

"I don't . . . maybe . . . my ribs . . . I don't know for sure," he said.

"Can you move?"

Feeling was slowly returning to Anton's extremities; he didn't think anything was broken, but his ribs hurt and his head was pounding. He tried moving his legs and arms. Nothing budged. He was completely pinned beneath the stones. He coughed to clear his throat of the dust and mud.

"I don't think so. The rocks are too heavy."

"Hold on!"

Daniel grunted and Anton heard the grinding sound of rocks sliding against one another above him. He tried again to move his legs and arms, but they were still stuck.

"Can you move now?" Daniel asked. Anton could tell that his friend was frightened.

"Daniel, I don't think I'm seriously injured. Be

careful that you do not hurt yourself. These rocks could still shift. I don't want you to get trapped, too."

Daniel did not answer. Anton could hear him straining as he struggled to move the stones between them. As the minutes passed, the ache in Anton's ribs worsened and he could only take short, shallow breaths.

"Anton, the rocks are too big for me lift by myself. I'm going to have to go back for help."

The thought scared Anton. He would be left alone in the dark and unable to move. Yet he could think of no other option. He tried to take a deep breath to calm himself, but the ache in his lungs made tranquility impossible. "Please hurry."

As Daniel scurried away, the sound of his footsteps faded into what felt like impenetrable silence.

But once Anton got used to the solitude, he began to notice things he would normally overlook. The drip of water on stone. The squish of mud beneath his legs. *Rustle. Swish. Flap.* He was not alone after all. He was sure he heard the skittering claws of a rat moving over the rocks above. Anton tried to remain calm, but the fact that he could not move terrified him.

He lurched his chest upward as hard as he could, straining to push the rocks off him, but it was no use. He would not be able to move without help. If the spot he had discovered, where the rocks had fallen, was a way to the surface, then rats and mice and snakes and all manner of creatures would use it to enter and leave the cave.

Something chirped in the darkness. *Skree! Skree!* He recognized the rat's call. They were plentiful in the granary and barn at home. Ordinarily, he would not give a rat a second thought. He'd set a trap or rely on the barn cat they had to keep the rats under control. But this was different.

Here he was flat on his back. If the rat had friends—which they usually did—they could make a meal of Anton at their leisure. Perhaps if he lay completely still, if he controlled his breathing, they would leave him alone.

Yet the more he attempted to remain calm, the more nervous he became. Sweat beaded on his forehead. He wished more than anything for a light so he could see his enemy before it attacked.

Skree, skree, skree, came the sound again. The rat was creeping closer.

"Stop!" Anton hissed. His voice was quickly swallowed up in echoes off the thick stone walls.

Skree, the rat replied. Anton wanted to shout, but he did not dare. What if a platoon of Nazis was patrolling above? No, he must be brave. It was only a rat, after all. It was not the gestapo. It was just a rat.

He pushed against the rocks that pinned down his feet, and somehow one of them actually moved! It was only a small crack, but to Anton it may as well have been an open door. The mud must have settled and freed some space. Working his right foot back and forth, he pushed again at the small boulder and moved it a little farther. Another push and the rock rolled off his foot. The lower half of his leg was free! Anton felt as if he had won a gold medal. Rock pushing was not an Olympic sport, but if it were, Anton would be the champion!

He placed his right foot on the rock pinning his left foot and pushed again. But this boulder was bigger. It wouldn't budge. He tried pressing his foot on the floor of the cave and pushing upward to see if he could slide the rocks off his upper body. The effort took every bit of energy he had. He strained and shoved, but nothing moved. He paused to catch his breath.

Skree!

He'd almost forgotten about the rat. At least his foot was now free. If the rat came close enough, he might be able to stomp it.

Anton had no idea how much time had passed. Surely, Daniel was coming back with help by now. A dark thought entered Anton's mind. What if Daniel had gotten lost? They had clearly marked the way, but Daniel was anxious in the best of circumstances. What if his fear distracted him into taking a wrong turn?

Skree. Skree.

Enough of this, Daniel thought to himself. He ground his teeth, put his right foot against the boulder pinning his left leg, and heaved with all his might. Just as he was about to give up, he felt the boulder move just a few millimeters.

"Yes!" he groaned.

Skree. He did not think the rat was cheering his success.

Taking a deep breath, he wedged his foot against the boulder again and shoved. The rock teetered for a moment, then rolled over. His left leg was free. It was cramped and shaking with exertion, but free.

"Praise God!" he sighed.

His upper body was still pinned. The rat was out there in the darkness somewhere. But he was winning. If only he could somehow get one of his arms free.

Skree.

"No, Mr. Rat," Anton whispered. "You will not make a meal of me."

Suddenly, another noise startled him. It was coming from farther down the passage. Footsteps.

"Anton! Anton!" Daniel called. "We are coming."

"It looks like you are outnumbered, Mr. Rat," Anton whispered. He heard the rat scamper away.

CHAPTER
TEN

Von Duesen and his squad crept carefully through the woods. The men they followed were unaware of their presence. The milk cans they carried clanked and squeaked on the wooden rail they hung from, masking the sound of the Germans' footsteps.

The two men stopped and set the cans on the ground. Von Duesen threw his fist up in the air, his elbow bent at a right angle. His men instantly came to a halt, guns at the ready. They watched and waited. Von Duesen wondered whether his excitement was clouding his judgment. Could the Jews have spotted them? If so, they might try to flee the mighty gestapo.

The major stood stock-still, he and his men statues in the darkness. The two Jews were about forty meters ahead. He heard them muttering softly, but could not hear well enough to understand what they were saying. In truth, it did not matter what they said. If they didn't lead him straight to their camp, they would soon be talking directly to him. They would tell him everything they knew about all the remaining Jews in the area. Major Karl Von Duesen was very good at interrogating prisoners.

The men picked up the milk cans and took off through the woods again. Sergeant Eberhardt looked at him, motioning to see if he wanted to grab the two men now. Von Duesen shook his head. He waved the men forward. These two would lead him to an entire group of hidden Jews. He would wait and capture them all.

For another fifteen minutes, they followed the men through the forest, listening to the milk cans clank against each other as they traversed the rough terrain. When the forest thinned out, Von Duesen gave his men the hand signal to stop again. They had reached a meadow and would need to be extra cautious crossing the open ground. All it would take for the Nazis to be exposed was one of the Jews glancing behind. He motioned his men together.

"Sergeant, stay with me," he whispered. "You two, stick to the tree line. One of you go left, the other right.

Circle around them. And make sure you are not spotted."

The two privates moved off through the trees. Von Duesen and Eberhardt watched the two *Juden* cross the meadow. They appeared completely unaware that they were being followed. When they'd gotten about a half a kilometer away, the meadow dipped. The Jews strolled down a hill and disappeared from sight.

Von Duesen touched Eberhardt on the arm. He raised a finger to his own lips, then motioned forward. "*Schnell,*" he whispered. *Hurry, but be quiet.* The major and the sergeant carried their machine guns at the ready. As quickly and quietly as they could, they sped forward. But as they approached the crest of the hill, Von Duesen stopped.

"*Herr* Major?" Eberhardt said, wondering why his commander had stopped so suddenly.

Karl Von Duesen was a believer. He believed in the Reich, the master race, that Jews were inferior in every way. It was inevitable that one day Germany would control the entire European continent. But he was also not stupid. He knew there were Jewish militias about. Armed militias. They lived deep in the forests and they raided German army posts, ambushed patrols, and even sent snipers to kill soldiers of the Reich. Their attempts were foolhardy and doomed to fail. But they did exist.

Major Karl Von Duesen would not walk blindly into a trap.

"Listen, Sergeant," he said.

Eberhardt concentrated, even cupping a hand to his right ear. He shook his head.

"I hear nothing, *mein* major," he whispered.

"Exactly," Von Duesen explained. "Where is the sound of the clanking milk cans?"

"Perhaps they are resting," the sergeant suggested.

"Perhaps," Von Duesen answered. "But perhaps they discovered we are following them and are waiting for us to show ourselves. We will not be ambushed."

"They did not appear to be carrying weapons, *Herr* Major," Eberhardt said.

"Appearances can get you killed, Sergeant. Never forget that. Spread out. We will approach the hilltop with twenty meters between us. If they are waiting, they will still expect us to be together. Move out," he said.

Sergeant Eberhardt dutifully moved off to his left.

When he was in position, they started forward. Von Duesen pulled back the slide on his machine gun, readying the weapon to fire. Quietly, they approached the hilltop. He took deep, regular breaths to steady his nerves.

The hill was really the edge of an old lake that had long ago dried up. The large depression in the ground was several hundred meters across and shaped roughly like a kidney. The bottom of the depression was littered with large boulders, shrubs, and a few small scrub trees that had barely managed to conquer the rocky soil.

Von Duesen and Eberhardt dropped to one knee at the top of the hill, as they had been trained, to make themselves the smallest targets possible. But as Major Von Duesen scanned the ground below, he saw no sign of the two Jews. Were they hiding among the rocks and bushes? Across the lake bed, something caught his eye and he raised his weapon. But it was only the two privates he had sent to the tree line. Clearly, they had not encountered the Jews, which meant they had to be close. They must be hiding down below, among the rocks and shrubs.

But where?

CHAPTER ELEVEN

It did not take long to free Anton. Daniel had returned with some of the older boys and several of the women, including the one named Rina whom Bubbe seemed to know. The passageway was narrow, but they managed to squeeze in and form a line. They wiggled and pulled at the rocks until they were loose enough to move, then passed them like a bucket brigade to get them out of Anton's way. One of the boys was named George and he worked like a demon, scrambling into the small spaces and clawing away at the rocks and mud. Within a few minutes, the last of the boulders had been pushed away and Anton could finally stand. Daniel helped him to feet.

"Ow!" Anton winced and grabbed his sides.

Rina took him by the shoulders. "Are you all right?" she asked.

"I don't know. My ribs ache. But only when I breathe," he said.

Rina took the flashlight Daniel had brought and shone it on Anton. He was covered from head to toe in mud and could not stand up completely straight.

"Help me get his coat off," Rina said to Daniel. As they carefully removed Anton's jacket, he groaned in pain.

"Show me where it hurts?" Rina asked.

Anton pointed to the spot on his right side and Rina's fingers probed the area.

"Ahh!" he groaned as her fingers continued running back and forth over his ribs. His eyes watered, but he did not cry out again.

"I do not think your ribs are broken, so that is good news. But they must be bruised quite badly. Can you walk?" she asked.

"I think so," he said.

Rina undid the long scarf—called a *babushka*—that concealed her hair, which was long and brown and reached the middle of her back.

"To be safe, let's wrap your ribs. It will keep them

from moving too much. When we return to the cavern, we can examine you more closely and make sure nothing is actually broken."

Anton nodded. Rina and a woman named Miriam wrapped the babushka snugly around his chest. When they tightened it, tying it into a knot, he thought he might pass out. He took a deep breath and held it until they had finished. When he let it out he found himself able to take only shallow breaths, but his ribs did not hurt as much.

"We should go now," Rina said.

The rest of the group turned away, ready to return to the cavern.

"Wait!" Anton said. "Daniel, the light, please?"

Daniel handed him the flashlight. Anton pointed it up to the ceiling. About a half meter over their heads, he saw the spot he had touched just before the rocks collapsed on him. He peered at a small hole in the ceiling that hadn't been there before.

Anton switched off the flashlight. It took a moment for everyone's eyes to adjust, but soon they could see the starlit skies above them. And the hole wasn't actually as small as it had first seemed. It was just big enough for a child to climb through. Flipping the light back on, Anton spied a rock the size of a watermelon sticking out of the side of the hole. Small beads of water ran down its sides and dripped into the passageway.

He tried to reach his hands over his head to grasp the rock, but the pain in his side was too great to continue. "Daniel, help me," he gasped.

"What are you doing?" Daniel asked.

"Uncle Dmitri wanted us to find another way out of the cave. If we widen this hole, and stack up some of these fallen rocks, we will have our exit," Anton said.

"We can do that later," Rina said. "Right now, you should be resting."

"But we can't know when we might need it," Anton said. "If we can just get this one rock out of the way, then stack up some of the stones like steps, we will be able to climb out at a moment's notice. Please. We are already here. We should finish the job." Anton looked at Daniel and Rina, his eyes pleading.

The two of them looked at each other, then shrugged. Anton watched as they grabbed hold of the large rock and pulled. It would not budge. They dug at the dirt surrounding it and tried again. It was wet and slippery, making it difficult for them to get a good grip.

They scraped at the dirt some more. "Be careful," Anton cautioned them. "Don't let it fall on you. Be ready."

Rina and Daniel kept digging until, without warning, the rock came loose from the soil holding it in place and crashed to the ground. Daniel and Rina lurched out of the way. It landed on the floor of the passageway with a *thud*. Anton flashed the light on the hole above them. It was now big enough for an adult to crawl through.

"Well done!" he said. "Now if we stack some of these rocks against the wall, like a staircase leading up—"

"We?" Daniel interrupted. "There is no *we* here, friend. There is us doing all the work and you giving us directions." His breath came in ragged gasps, but he was smiling.

Anton chuckled. "True, but at least I do not creep down the passageways like a frightened squirrel."

Daniel playfully punched him on the shoulder. It made Anton wince, but he was glad of it. Daniel had been so quiet and reserved since they'd arrived at the cave. It was good to see him smiling.

The group went to work. The women and boys formed another line in the narrow passageway and returned the fallen rocks that had trapped Anton one by one to Rina and Daniel. Carefully, the two of them stacked the stones against the wall. They scooped mud from the tunnel floor to help support the rocks, and soon they had a makeshift stairway. It would take some careful climbing to reach the hole above, but it was better than nothing.

When they were finished, Anton inspected their work. "Excellent. Now we will be able to reach the surface if we need to. Uncle Dmitri will be pleased. Perhaps they will find a ladder on one of their night missions, and we can it bring here. Until then, this will work well."

Rina and Daniel smiled. The group finally headed back down the passageway, with Daniel in the lead, lighting the way with his flashlight. They were tired and dirty. Anton winced with each step. But he was happy to have done what his uncle had asked of him. Even if it hadn't gone exactly the way he had planned.

Now if the gestapo comes we will be ready for them, he thought to himself as he limped along.

We will be ready.

CHAPTER TWELVE

Major Von Duesen and his men waited at the edge of the depression for several minutes. They strained to hear the two men they'd been following. Had they stopped to rest or to catch a field mouse for supper? Von Duesen had no idea. Only the sound of his own ragged breathing disturbed the silence. Where were they? The dried pond was not that big and the moon was bright. He should be able to see them!

Sergeant Eberhardt returned to his side.

"*Mein* major?" he asked.

"*Sie müssen Geister sein*, Sergeant," Von Duesen said. *They must be ghosts.*

He studied the terrain. In truth, there were many places for two men to hide. Perhaps they had realized they were being followed and hidden among the rocks and bushes. Motioning to his men on the opposite side, Von Duesen gestured for them to go down into the depression and search for their quarry.

"Forward, Sergeant," he said. "We will comb the area. The *Juden* are here. I am certain of it. But be careful. They could be armed."

The two men crept slowly down the incline, their machine guns held at the waist, ready to fire. If the fugitives tried anything, they would be cut down like a scythe slashing through wheat. The Germans moved cautiously and quietly.

Working as a team, they investigated each rock and tree, each cluster of bushes and copse of trees. But so far the men were nowhere to be found. It was as if they had turned to mist and faded away. Von Duesen watched his two privates working their way toward him. They moved in concert, just as he and Eberhardt did, making sure each possible hiding place was clear before moving on.

Several more minutes passed. Periodically, Von Duesen would signal the squad to halt, so they could listen for the rustling of clothing, the gasp of a breath, the beat of a heart. But he heard nothing. Von Duesen was baffled.

One hundred meters remained between the major and his two privates. The ground was rocky, the boulders that littered it large. If the *Juden* were still here, this would be where they were hiding.

"Be ready, Sergeant," he whispered.

"*Ja*," Eberhardt answered.

A boulder nearly the size of an automobile stood directly ahead of them. Von Duesen went left and Eberhardt to the right. They leapt around the boulder, guns at the ready. But the Jews were not there. Behind them they heard a rustle in the bushes. Von Duesen turned quickly, prepared to fire. But before he could pull the trigger, a large hare bolted from the underbrush and darted away.

Von Duesen took a breath to calm his nerves. Silently, he cursed himself. A soldier of the Reich did not jump in fear at the appearance of a rabbit. A gestapo major was not afraid of two Jewish peasants. This was ridiculous. He needed to remain calm. And to find what he was looking for.

He waved his gun, motioning Eberhardt forward. Another large boulder lay ahead of them, and they repeated their crawl around it. Von Duesen peered around the opposite side of the boulder expecting to find two huddling Jews. But that was not what awaited him.

Sitting on the ground were two milk cans. The very ones the two *Juden* had been carrying. Von Duesen kicked one of them as hard as he could. Water spilled out and ran through the dirt in tiny rivulets. Just as he feared, his squad had been discovered.

But where had the Jews gone? They had to be somewhere.

His men joined him at the giant boulder. They looked at the milk cans and then at the major with disbelief on their faces.

"Did you see anything?" Von Duesen demanded.

"No, *mein* major," they answered in unison.

Von Duesen paced back and forth. Somehow, he had been outwitted. He had figured out where the fugitives were, yet they still managed to elude him. When he finally caught them he would make them wish they had never been born. They would tell him everything. Everything. They would reveal the location of every Jew in the entire area.

"Tomorrow," Von Duesen said. "Tomorrow, we come back during the morning hours. We will bring additional men and search every stone and shrub in this area. We will find out how these *Juden* managed to escape the gestapo. Is that understood?"

"*Ja, mein* major," his squad answered.

"Heil Hitler!" Von Duesen said, giving the Nazi salute, which his men returned.

Von Duesen clenched his fists, turned, and retreated, his men struggling to keep up with their superior. The empty milk cans watched them go.

CHAPTER
THIRTEEN

Bubbe's long, bony fingers probed Anton's side. He tried not to flinch, but a sharp intake of breath gave him away.

"*Ach*," his grandmother said. "They do not feel broken, but Rina was right. They are badly bruised. You will need to keep them wrapped while they heal. And you must try to rest. No running off with Daniel." She dipped a cloth in a pail of water, wrung it out, then dabbed at his face.

"Please, Bubbe," he said. "I can do it myself." He took the cloth and wiped the mud from his face. He was filthy, but there was not enough water in the camp for him to take a bath. So he'd just have to make do.

The peace in the cavern was soon disturbed when Uncle Dmitri and one of the other men came barreling in. The man's name was on the tip of Anton's tongue. He had not gotten to know everyone yet. He searched his memory. Slava. The man's name was Slava. Sweat dripped from his brow, and both he and Uncle Dmitri were breathless.

His uncle stopped, bent over, and placed his hands on his knees.

"Dmitri, my son," Bubbe said. "What is wrong?" Bubbe was the eldest in the cave, and since they had arrived, she had done her best to keep the group calm and busy. But now, Anton could hear that her voice was filled with worry, though she was trying not to show it.

"We were followed from the stream," Dmitri said. "Somehow, the gestapo discovered our water source. Four of them followed us. We lost them among the boulders. But it was close. They know we are somewhere nearby. They will either wait us out, or they will return with more men to search for our hiding place."

"What shall we do?" Bubbe asked.

"We dare not go out again tonight. If they left a man behind to stand guard, we will be captured. It is only a few hours to daylight. And we must not venture out then, either," Dmitri said.

Everyone was quiet. The silence in the cave unnerved Anton. He had felt safe here, and now he felt anything but.

Dmitri straightened up. "We will block the entrance. Try to camouflage it somehow so they will overlook it. We will have to cut down on rations while we wait to see if they give up the search. Anton, did you find another exit?"

"Yes, Uncle," Anton said. "The way is marked." He explained to Dmitri what they had discovered. Dmitri smiled and clapped him on the shoulder. The pain from his ribs nearly brought Anton to his knees.

"Well done, lad. We may need to use it. Everyone gather up a bag of essentials. Have it near you and ready to go. If the gestapo comes for us they will force their way through this entrance."

"Why don't we just leave now? Go out the back way?" Anton asked.

Dmitri shook his head. "What if they are still out there? We do not know exactly where your exit will let us out. No, for now we will wait. They will begin their search at the spot where Slava and I disappeared. If they find the entrance to this cave, they will storm it. Then we will slip out the back, where they are not looking."

Anton thought about the plan. They would wait and see. It made sense.

The German army had a way of popping up unexpectedly.

FOURTEEN

The entrance to the cave had been well camouflaged. The gestapo did not show up the next day. Or the one after that. Yet Dmitri and the other men refused to leave the cave. Water had to be rationed. In another day or so they would run completely out and would have no choice but to go in search of more.

While they waited, they worked on their exit strategy. Anton led Uncle Dmitri, Sergei, and Slava to the primitive staircase in the tunnel. The men improved the base and constructed a ladder from some lumber they had salvaged on one of their nighttime runs. Now everyone would be able to quickly climb out if they needed to escape.

The rest of the time, the group rested. They had to conserve both food and energy. It was boring, but it did wonders for Anton's ribs. His sides still hurt when he laughed or coughed, but soon he could breathe and move freely.

The monotony only seemed to make everyone else more nervous. The men took turns guarding the narrow opening that led to the cave entrance. Each hour they waited, the tension grew. Anton let himself believe the danger was past. On the third night, when they were nearly out of water, Uncle Dmitri decided they needed to risk venturing out of the cave.

They split up into three teams of two men. Two of the teams would go to the river—one upstream, the other down. The third team would travel farther, to a small spring about three kilometers north of the cave.

"Dmitri, this is not a good plan," Bubbe said. "What if the gestapo is watching? Even if they did not find our cave, they could still be waiting nearby to ambush us."

Dmitri shook his head. "Mama, we can wait no longer. The children are thirsty. We need water to cook. There is no other option."

The men readied themselves for the mission, putting on their warm coats and gloves. They all wore dark clothes and covered their faces in mud. No one wanted to be given away by moonlight. Each man grabbed a tin milk can, and they steeled themselves for the night ahead.

But before they could leave, a small metal cylinder clattered down the rock-lined entrance to the cave. Anton heard an earsplitting pop. Smoke began to pour out of the cylinder, filling the chamber.

"Grenade!" Dmitri yelled. "Everyone! To the tunnel! Take only what you can car—" His words were cut off by the sound of machine-gun fire. Bullets flew, ricocheting off the stone walls.

"Hurry!" Dmitri pleaded. The cave became a flurry of activity as everyone scattered about, gathering up their meager possessions.

"To the tunnel!" he said.

Anton grabbed his bag and glanced around for Bubbe. Uncle Dmitri had made her his responsibility if someone should uncover their hiding place. She stood near the entrance of the cave, her walking stick in hand. Looking over his shoulder, Anton saw that most of the group was disappearing into the darkness of the tunnel. Daniel waved for him to follow, but Anton had to get to Bubbe.

Only she isn't moving, he thought. *Why isn't she*

moving? If we don't get out of here, the gestapo is going to get us, and all of this will have been for nothing!

But suddenly, he realized what she was doing. If Bubbe remained behind, the Nazis would have to deal with her, which would give everyone else time to get away.

Anton lunged forward and grabbed her arm. "Bubbe, come! We must hurry."

The gunshots had stopped, but the echo of boots and the shouts of "*Schnell*" and "*Halten*" were coming closer.

"No, Anton," she said. "You must go. Help your uncle lead the others to the Priest's Grotto. I am old and weak, and I will only slow the group down."

"But, Bubbe," Anton said, his eyes filling with tears. "You will be taken to the camps, or—"

The footsteps were drawing nearer. By now, the cavern was empty except for Rina and her small son, David, who appeared too frightened to move. He grabbed a small pillar of rock and hugged it tightly as she pulled at his arms and pleaded with him to come with her.

"Bubbe. Please!" Anton begged.

"Listen to your bubbe. Run. Help the others."

"No, Bubbe! I won't leave you!" Anton did not know what to do. Seconds ticked by, each one measured by the pounding of his heart.

"They are coming, Anton. Hide! God will watch over me." She pushed him away. The soldiers were in the entrance tunnel now. There was not enough time for Anton to run. He looked around wildly. A small, dark depression in the wall a few meters away caught his eye. A wooden table one of the men had constructed stood in front of it, masking the opening in shadow. Anton ran to it and crawled inside, making himself as small as possible. Rina had managed to pry her son away from the column, but she had no chance to race to the tunnel before a squad of German soldiers entered the chamber.

It was easy to recognize their gestapo uniforms. All of them carried machine guns, except for the lead officer, who pointed a Luger—a large and powerful pistol—right at Bubbe. Anton nearly lunged from his hiding place. He wanted desperately to put himself between Bubbe and the barrel of the gun. As if she were reading his mind, she tapped the ground twice with her walking stick, reminding him and everyone else who might hear it to be quiet and pay attention.

The officer squinted at her cane. He was very young. As Anton studied him, he memorized the man's features. His chin was sharp, almost pointed. His nose was slightly small for his face. Blond hair peeked out from beneath his uniform cap, and even at this distance, the icy blueness of his eyes shone in the flickering light of the lanterns. His uniform was immaculate except for a bit of mud on his boots. Uncle Dmitri had taught Anton to recognize the ranks of German officers. Major's braids adorned his collar. Anton felt a fluttering of fear in his stomach. How could one so young rise to such a rank? It must be because he was ruthless and cruel.

The major stared at Bubbe. She stared back at him unflinchingly. If he thought he could win a staring contest with her, *Herr* Major was in for a rude awakening. Though she was old and bent by the harshness of her life, there remained steel in her. She had needed it to survive and raise her sons when Anton's grandfather passed. Her face showed no fear—only resolve. The officer looked away first, his gaze jumping all around the chamber before settling on Rina and her child. The major barked an order.

Anton understood some German and believed he'd told one of his men to take Rina away.

"*Nein*," Bubbe said. *No.*

The officer looked at the old woman standing in front of him, his face a mixture of anger and bemusement.

"*Nein?*" he asked, laughing.

Bubbe nodded. "*Nein.* We are living here in peace. We bother no one. You have no right to take us anywhere."

"I have every right," the major said. "The führer has annexed this land and declared it *Judenfrei*. It is the law."

"Annexed? Don't you mean conquered?" Bubbe threw back her head and laughed. "What have you conquered, exactly? From all we hear, the mighty German army could not take a single city in Russia. In fact, the word is your military is retreating from the eastern front. And what exactly have you conquered here? An old woman, a mother, and her baby?"

Anger flashed in the major's eyes and Anton wished she would not antagonize a man holding a gun. But he also knew that every moment she kept the soldiers here in the cave bought time for the others to escape. *Please, Bubbe,* he prayed. *Please be careful.*

"You are under arrest. You will be taken into custody and transported to Borta, where you will be processed. You will come peacefully or—if you wish—we can force you. The führer does not care how the *Juden* are taken, only that they are."

"Ah. Yes, your mighty führer," Bubbe said. "What is he so afraid of? His war cannot be won unless he captures farmers and cobblers and blacksmiths? Do these simple people cause the mighty Reich to cower in fear?"

The major's hand snapped out like a snake and struck Bubbe across the face. Even as he did so, she tapped her walking stick twice on the chamber floor. She knew Anton was watching and wanted him to remain hidden. She took the slap stoically, refusing to acknowledge the humiliation . . . or the pain.

"I see the Reich is very good at teaching the gestapo how to beat up old women," she said. "If you would like, I can take you to all the nearby houses with defenseless, elderly women so you can slap them around as well."

The major raised his hand again, but this time something made him stop. She was goading him. "You will find that righteous attitude and sharp tongue will be of little use to you in the camps," he said.

"You are very brave, *Herr* Major. Tell me, what type of medal do you get for capturing an old woman?"

The major ignored her insult. He turned to his men. "Take them," he said. "The rest of you search this chamber. There must be more of them hidden here somewhere."

Anton wanted to cry out. He wished more than anything that he were older and stronger. If he were, he would dive from his hiding place, grab the major's gun, and shoot all the Germans dead. He would move like lightning, killing them all before they had a chance to react.

But Anton was just a boy. So instead, he watched in horror as the soldiers grabbed Bubbe roughly by the arms and dragged her toward the entrance to the cave.

Rina clasped her sobbing, terrified son to her chest, but the men did not care. One of them roughly pushed her forward, and she stumbled and nearly fell.

"Schnell! Schnell!" he hollered at her. Another soldier ripped David from her arms. The small boy screamed in terror, his tiny arms reaching out for his mother.

"No! Please, no!" Rina cried. Another one of the soldiers drove the butt of his rifle into her stomach. She gasped in agony, and would have collapsed to the ground if he had not caught her and dragged her along.

Anton cowered in the darkness until they disappeared from sight. He felt ashamed that he had not rushed to their aid. But now all he could do was pray that the remaining soldiers would not find him here in the darkness. If he managed to elude them, he was not sure what would come next. Should he try to catch up with the others on their way to the Priest's Grotto? No, he could not leave Bubbe in the hands of the Nazis. It was a horrible feeling, not knowing what to do.

He could only hope that God would give him the chance to escape the cave . . . and to rescue his grandmother.

CHAPTER FIFTEEN

Anton waited until the cavern was empty.

Watching the major and four of his men take Bubbe, Rina, and David away had been excruciating. He wondered if the gestapo had a vehicle on the surface to carry Bubbe away or if they would make her take the long walk to the nearest road. The other soldiers split up into groups of two and disappeared, heading in every direction to search the cavern's many tunnels. He hoped they wouldn't spot the markers he and Daniel had drawn.

After a few long minutes, Anton crawled out from his hiding place as quietly as he could. He strung his blanket bag over his shoulder and crept silently to the tunnel entrance. He did not dare use a lantern or flashlight. Pausing, he listened for the sound of retreating soldiers.

When he was certain he was alone, he scurried up the tunnel to the cave's entrance. The starlight was a welcome sight. But he couldn't dally here. He had to find Bubbe. The view in front of him was pockmarked with boulders and far too rocky for a vehicle to get close. But off to the east, toward the river, he heard the sound of an engine. He studied the surrounding terrain. There were no soldiers in sight.

As quickly as he could, he darted in the direction of the revving engine, using the boulders for cover. Several meters away, he spotted a half-track idling along the riverbank. In the distance he could see Bubbe and Rina being loaded roughly into the back of the gray metal military vehicle, the giant black swastika painted on its side a grim reminder of the monsters who controlled their fate.

The half-track pulled away and traveled slowly along the river. Anton broke into a run. They would not be able to drive at full speed until they reached the nearest road. He should be able to keep up with them. Perhaps if he could get ahead of them, he could find a way to stop the vehicle. If he could get the Germans to abandon it and force them to walk, he'd have a better chance of freeing Bubbe. It was risky. And it wasn't even a plan. Not really. But it was the only thing he could think of. He wished Uncle Dmitri were with him. He would know what to do.

The major had said the prisoners were being taken to Borta to be interrogated. Borta was many kilometers from the cave. He would need to stop them before they reached it.

Taking one last look to be sure no other gestapo were about, Anton sprinted from the cover of the rocks and followed the half-track into the night. His ribs were still sore, and each step sent a little jolt of pain through his side. But he pushed it from his mind. He *would* follow them and find a way to get Bubbe back. Rina and her son, too. He would get them all back.

As he ran along, he wondered what had happened to the rest of the group. How would they get to the Priest's Grotto? If his half-a-plan was successful, how would they catch up?

One thing at a time, Anton, he told himself.

The ground was rough and he stumbled several times as he ran, but he managed to keep the half-track in sight. He wished he could use the flashlight he'd stashed in his bag, but he couldn't risk it. He tripped over a rock and fell headlong onto the hard ground, scraping his hands and knees. It felt as if a knife had been driven into his ribs. He wanted to cry out in pain, but would not allow himself. He took a moment to catch his breath, then clambered to his feet and got back to running after the half-track.

They had now reached the potato fields that ran along the river bottom. Soon, the half-track would reach the road. When that happened he would no longer be able to keep up. But he had an idea.

They would have to drive north on the road until it joined a larger one that led directly to Borta. If he cut across the field, he could intercept them. Anton turned and ran, keeping the half-track on his left. His breath caught as it disappeared behind some trees. So he pushed himself harder, cutting diagonally across the field. As the half-track emerged from behind the trees, it slowed. A bright searchlight from its roof cut through the night.

Anton assumed they might be looking for other members of his party. The half-track crawled slowly along the road now. This was his chance. He knew that the searchlight could find him, so he sped up, charging through the field as fast as his legs would carry him. He had no idea how he would stop them, but he had to try.

When he reached the edge of the field, he noticed a small shed. The potato farmer who owned it would keep his equipment there. If Anton could get inside, he might find something he could use to stop the half-track. But when he ran around the small shed to the door, his heart sank. It was padlocked shut.

Anton examined the lock. It was old and rusty. He dropped to his hands and knees and felt around until he found a rock the size of his fist. He worried about the noise he was about to make. But there was no time to dwell on it. He smashed the rock against the lock. It held. Again he swung, and again the lock would not budge. The third time, he raised his arm high over his head and brought the rock down on the lock. It broke open!

Scrambling inside the shed, he pulled the door closed, grabbed the flashlight from his pack, and flicked it on. He'd found a treasure trove. There were shovels and hoes and scythes. The walls were lined with hammers and wrenches. But he couldn't see anything that might help him stop the half-track.

Shining the light into all corners of the windowless shed, he saw a shelf on the back wall that held several cans. He pulled each one off and examined the contents. They held nuts and bolts and other small hardware. The last can was the biggest. It was heavy, and when he looked inside he nearly leapt for joy. It was full of rusty nails—hundreds of them. And they gave him a very good idea.

He tucked the can under his arm, raced out of the shed, and headed for the road.

CHAPTER SIXTEEN

Major Von Duesen could not have been happier. He had found where the *Juden* were hiding! He was returning with prisoners and he had no doubt his men would collect more. He had rooted them out, and now the Jews were cowering like rats.

He looked at the old woman sitting on the floor of the half-track's bed. She had done her best to insult him, to belittle the führer. He looked forward to her interrogation. They would see how proud she was then. Her foolish resistance would not stand against the might of the gestapo. The other woman was young and strong, and would likely be sent to one of the Reich's factories. She would work long hours sewing uniforms or operating machines to build bombs or bullets. When she had been worked to exhaustion, they would send her to one of the camps. He had no idea what would happen to her child, nor did he care.

But he did care about reaching the road. The half-track bumped over the rocky ground, turning the major's stomach. They traveled slowly through the fields until finally they reached the road, where the ride smoothed out. When the engine quieted, he could hear the old woman muttering curses under her breath. He kicked her hard in the leg.

"What is the matter, *Jude*?" he snarled. "Do you have nothing to say now that you are a prisoner? Now that you are the property of the Reich?"

The old woman spat at him. Spittle flew from her mouth and landed on his boots. He raised his hand to strike her, but stopped when he saw that she was not afraid and stared at him with complete defiance. That was what she wanted. She would take the beatings if it meant distracting him from learning about the rest of the hidden *Juden*. He would not give her that satisfaction. Yet. But eventually she would fold. Everyone had a breaking point.

"Curse all you want, old woman," he said. "Pray to your God. Nothing is going to help you now." To his surprise, the old woman studied him for what seemed like several minutes. Her eyes narrowed and her brow furrowed before she finally spoke.

"You can't hide it," she told him. The expression on her face changed from one of concentration to a derisive sneer.

"Hide what?"

"Your fear."

Von Duesen threw back his head and laughed. The old woman glared as she reached over to the young woman and her child and placed her arm around them.

"My fear?" he said. "You believe I am afraid of two women and a child? Are you insane?"

"No. You are not afraid of me. You are a bully and a coward, but you are not afraid of a tired old woman. You, *Herr* Major, are afraid of losing."

"Losing? Losing what? Trust me, old woman, I will not lose you. And if you try to escape I will not hesitate to shoot you down like a dog."

Now it was the old woman's turn to throw back her head and laugh.

"You Germans. Such zealots. So self-righteous. You

are nothing more than the puppets of a madman. And you cannot see the truth, even when it is right before your eyes."

"And what truth would that be?"

"You are losing. Your kind always loses."

"What great failure is befalling the Reich, *Jude*?"

"Your fear drips off of you. You are losing the war. You know it. Your führer knows it. He sends you out to gather up the Jews. You think us weak and simple. But we know things. The Americans have joined the British, and soon they will gather their forces. In the east, the Russian army chases you back to Rhineland with your tails between your legs. And with the Americans coming from the west, where is the mighty Reich? Right in the middle, waiting to be squashed like a bug.

"And yet your mighty führer wastes his time and resources rounding up poor peasants and farmers. Does this make sense to you, *Herr* Major? Shouldn't the führer be readying himself for the storm that is about to descend upon him? Would that not be a better plan?"

"Ha! I give you credit, old woman. You are not afraid to speak your mind." His eyes narrowed. "Perhaps I should take you to the führer himself so he can listen to you tell him how to fight a war."

"Perhaps you should."

"The Reich will not be defeated. Do not worry, Jew. You will not live to see a free day again. The führer will smash the Americans and the British. And your mighty Russian army has been reduced to women, children, and feeble old men. They will never reach the Rhineland. When the time is right, we will crush them."

The old woman raised her hand. "Of course. It worked so well for you in Stalingrad. The Russians are not fighting with their strongest men, and still you could not conquer them. And then there are the Americans. You think they will ever stop until you are defeated? They have millions of men to send. Millions. How many does the Reich have left? A few hundred thousand? How long before your mighty gestapo is in shambles? Do not try to lie to me, *Herr* Major. Your eyes give you away."

For reasons he did not understand, this bent, beaten old woman, with her walking stick and her peasant clothes and her wrinkled face, had unnerved him. How did she know so much about the humiliation the Reich had suffered against the communist pigs in Russia? The Reich had been driven out of Africa. The Americans were on the march in Italy, gaining more and more ground. How could she know that the führer was desperately sending reinforcements to the French coast, building bunkers and gun emplacements, as he waited for the imminent invasion? Before he could answer, the half-track slowed. Sergeant Eberhardt turned on the searchlight and swept it across the road in front of them.

"What is it, Sergeant?" he asked.

"I'm not sure, *mein* major. Perhaps nothing. I thought I spotted something in the road ahead. Perhaps it is one of the *Juden* from the cave."

"Stop the truck. Turn off the engine," he ordered, pulling the Luger from the holster at his belt. He used a machine gun when necessary, but nothing felt as good as the weight of his trusty pistol in his hand. The beam of light danced over the road ahead and into the fields on either side.

"Perhaps this time you will catch an infant."

"Shut up, *Jude*, or you will regret it."

Unafraid of Von Duesen's threat, the old woman staggered to her feet and shouted, "If you are out there, go to the shadows, they will not fin—" A blow to her face knocked her to the floor of the half-track. The young woman screamed and her son began to wail. Von Duesen pointed his pistol at them. "Silence. Silence now or the boy dies."

She grabbed her son and pulled him tightly against her chest. She quietly pleaded with him to quiet. He buried his face in her coat as the old woman moaned in pain.

"Ahead, slowly," Von Duesen ordered. The driver restarted the half-track and now it crawled along the road. The spotlight swept back and forth, searching for any sign of life. But there was nothing to see.

After a short distance, Von Duesen ordered the driver to speed up.

"Perhaps you saw an animal, Sergeant," said Von Duesen. "Or maybe the shadows are playing tricks on your eyes."

"*Mein* major, I think I saw—"

He did not get a chance to finish. Both of the front tires on the half-track exploded with a loud bang. The vehicle swerved, tossing the men about. The driver fought for control and lost as the half-track careened off the road and into the field. It skidded to a stop, and began to sink into the muddy ground.

SEVENTEEN

The half-track had been a half a kilometer away when Anton had reached the edge of the road. Carefully, he'd grabbed small handfuls of nails and tossed them around the path until it was covered. The nails were darkened by rust and blended in well with the dirt road. He set the can down and retreated back into the field. Now he would watch and wait.

He watched as the half-track approached. It had two front rubber tires like a truck, but the rear was powered by metal treads like those found on a tank. The rear of the vehicle was open like a truck bed, and there was a searchlight and a machine gun mounted on the roof of the cab. Anton would not be able to destroy the treads, but if he could flatten the rubber tires, it would be impossible to steer.

Anton held his breath. It would be entirely possible for the half-track to roll right over the nails without a problem. It would require luck for one of them to pierce the tires. But this was his only plan. If the gestapo made it to the road to Borta, he would never be able to keep up. He would lose Bubbe.

Two loud popping sounds cut through the night air, and the half-track pitched to the right. It had worked! Both front tires went flat and the driver lost control of the vehicle. It bounced off the road and into the potato field, where it lurched to a stop and sank in the soft soil.

"Was ist passiert?" the major shouted. *What happened?* He issued another command and the four soldiers exited the vehicle and took up positions around the half-track, their guns at the ready. Anton thought the Germans looked as if they were about to be attacked by one of the militias or Ukrainian partisans. If they only knew they'd been felled by a twelve-year-old boy!

"Ausbreiten! Ausbreiten!" the major shouted. Each man chose a direction and crept cautiously forward.

Anton knew he was lucky. Now that the men had stopped, they were nervous and could not risk turning on the searchlight for fear of making themselves a target. He watched as the soldiers spread out, carefully moving away from the half-track. One of them was headed right toward Anton. He could see the man silhouetted against the night sky. And the Nazi was not deviating from his course.

What could Anton do? He dared not move. He had no weapon, no way to defend himself. In another thirty meters, the soldier would run right into him.

Anton curled inward, pulling his arms and legs close to himself. He offered up a silent prayer and buried his face. Whatever happened now was out of his hands. As he waited, he could hear the soldier's footsteps drawing closer. He would not lift his head to see how close the man was. If he looked he might be spotted, and if he was spotted he would surely be gunned down.

Sweat soaked his clothes. It took all his concentration to control his breathing. His nose itched and he longed to scratch it, but any movement now could spell death. Dry weeds and twigs crunched beneath the soldier's feet. Each step sounded like a cannon shot. Anton guessed the man was no farther than ten meters away now. Every muscle in his body tensed as he waited for discovery. He braced for the gunshot that would surely come. *I'm sorry, Bubbe,* he thought to himself. *I tried. I did not know what else to do. Please forgive me.*

"*Halten,*" he heard the major shout. "*Kommen Sie.*" The major was ordering the men to return to the half-track. Slowly and cautiously, Anton raised his head and saw the back of the soldier who had been about to trip over him only moments earlier. The major stood next to the vehicle, with Bubbe, Rina, and David clustered nearby.

Quietly, Anton rose to his hands and knees and crept toward the group. He needed to hear what the major would do next. Most likely, he would radio to Borta for another truck to come pick them up. But he did not think the major was stupid. In fact, he was counting on it. A smart man would start walking toward Borta and have the truck meet them on the road. Waiting here, they were exposed.

The major and his men discussed what to do. Bubbe, Rina, and David huddled off to the side. The men spoke loudly, and Anton used the noise of their voices to cover his approach. He was close enough to hear them clearly now. They were speaking quickly, but he managed to understand that they had radioed for someone to pick them up, but there were no available vehicles at the moment.

Anton thought about what he should do now. He had been focused on stopping the half-track, but now that he had done that, he didn't know what to do next. He would need to think of another way to distract them, something to make them forget about Bubbe long enough to spirit her away. Morning was coming soon. He needed to work quickly.

The major barked out an order, and the group started marching. In single file, he took the lead. Two of his men followed behind him, Bubbe, Rina, and David after that, then the other two men brought up the rear. They marched along the road, and Anton's heart leapt at the sight of Bubbe's shadow. Her body bent at the waist and her ever-present walking stick tapped the ground with every shuffling step. He knew she was old, but he also realized that Bubbe would do anything to slow them down, delay them, or otherwise cause trouble. But that came with consequences. And it was why Anton ached to get her away from the gestapo before more of them showed up and his options dwindled.

When they had traveled a safe distance, Anton rose and began to follow them. But he stayed in the field—if one of the soldiers suddenly looked behind them, Anton didn't want to be seen.

A few minutes later, the group reached the road toward Borta and turned, with Anton at their heels. As he walked, he tried desperately to come up with a plan to free his grandmother.

He was running out of time.

CHAPTER EIGHTEEN

Major Von Duesen was angry beyond belief. He was also on high alert. Someone had sabotaged his vehicle. He suspected that a partisan patrol had seen the half-track and used the opportunity to take it out. Now they were lurking in the darkness.

He had radioed to command in Borta. They would send another truck as soon as one was available. But in the meantime, he and his team were exposed. He had argued with his sergeant about what to do next. Eberhardt hadn't wanted to leave the cover of the half-track, with its machine gun and searchlight. But Von Duesen worried about snipers. The half-track made them a target. It was better to head to Borta and let another unit recover the vehicle later.

Still, he would not let the sabotage of the half-track interfere with the joy he felt at all he had accomplished this evening. He had rooted out an entire encampment of Jews and taken three prisoners. He was sure his men would round up the others. Yet as he replayed in his mind the conversation he'd had with the old woman, he could not help but let a little doubt creep in. The news of the Reich's humiliation in Russia, especially at Stalingrad, was now spreading. This was not good. As the führer always said, they must not allow the enemy, especially *Juden*, to have hope.

Though the German army had done great damage to the Russian war machine, they had not been able to defeat the Russian people. Even the Luftwaffe, the great German air force, had been unable to bring them to heel. He had not lied when he said that the Russians had used women, children, and old men to fight. His brother Heinz's letters had said that some of the most fearsome snipers in Stalingrad were women. He said the soldiers moved through the city by fighting in one house, then the next house. Heinz would joke that today they had "taken the parlor and the dining room, but the Russians still held the kitchen."

Last night he had reread the most recent note he had received from Heinz.

Karl,

I realize it has been some time since I have written and though I am exhausted from the fighting, I owe you a letter. Where to begin? I hope the censors will not read this, but what can I do to stop them? We are near defeat. The Russians will not give up. We are running out of ammo, food, and clothing. The winter freezes us to our bones, yet we fight on in the name of the führer. But not even the mighty Luftwaffe has been able to break the Russian spirit.

We have heard that Russian infantry officers are shooting anyone who attempts to retreat on the spot. How can such a people be defeated? Yesterday we fought in a house in Stalingrad against a Russian squad with nothing more than bayonets. The fighting was brutal, exhausting. The Russians cursed us as we retreated.

This was a mistake, Karl. We should never have come here. We have lost so many men and now there is talk that we must surrender. Our tanks are out of fuel, our planes will not fly in the cold. I am afraid it is too late for us. And

what will happen when the Americans land in
the west? We cannot be everywhere at once, Karl.
    Remember that and be careful, wherever
your duty may take you.

Your brother,
Heinz

That was the last he had heard from Heinz in months. Another gestapo officer had told Karl that he'd heard Heinz's squadron were all prisoners in a camp somewhere in frozen Siberia. Karl wondered whether he would ever see his brother again.

But he could not dwell on such personal matters. One man's life was nothing if it meant success for the führer and for Germany. But Karl could see no success on the eastern front. The defeat in Russia had weakened the Reich. So many men captured! And now that horrible news had spread through the countryside. Karl could not imagine how it had happened. Most of these peasants could not afford radios, and yet the old woman knew so much.

It must have been the work of the partisan militias

that patrolled the countryside and aligned themselves with the Russian army. But in the end, how the old woman knew did not really matter. Only that her information was correct. And it worried him.

He had heard rumblings from the top commanders. Many had questioned the führer's decision to invade Russia. He wanted their oil fields, their resources. But Russia had so many more men than the Reich, and the German forces were already spread thin. The Americans had taken southern Italy and were pushing northward. The cowardly Italians had already surrendered. To invade Russia—with its rugged terrain, horrible winters, and stubborn refusal to be beaten—called the führer's judgment into question.

Von Duesen heard Eberhardt shout at the old woman. He turned in time to see the man roughly shove her forward. She stumbled and fell to the ground.

"*Was passiert ist*, Sergeant?" he asked. *What is going on here?*

"This biddy cannot keep up. She is too old and too slow. We should just shoot her," Eberhardt said as he raised his gun and pointed it at her.

Even now, she shows no fear, Von Duesen marveled.

She may have been *Juden*, but a small part of him admired her defiance.

"Get up," he said.

"No. My bones ache. I cannot walk any further."

"You will get up and you will walk or you will be shot," Von Duesen said. He removed the Luger pistol from his holster and pointed it at her forehead. "Now get up. Do not think I do not know what you are up to, you old crone. You are doing everything in your power to delay us to give the other *Juden* time to escape. Your tactics are useless. We will catch them. They will suffer. Just as you are going to suffer. Now get up."

"No," the old woman said.

Von Duesen cocked the hammer on the Luger.

"Get up!"

"No."

"I swear, old woman—"

To his amazement she laughed at him. "Do you think I fear death, *Herr* Major? I have made my peace with God. You will not shoot me. Not yet. Not when you think you can torture me into revealing where my friends and family are. You are not done with me yet, *Herr* Major. You will not pull the trigger."

Von Duesen considered her words.

"You are right, Madam. I do expect you to tell me everything about the *Juden* in this area. So I will not shoot you." Von Duesen smiled and shifted his arm until the Luger was pointed at the boy.

"But the boy," he said. "He knows nothing. I can shoot him. The Reich has no use for him. And he slows us down as much as you do. So what do you say now, old woman? Where is your bravery and indignation when the gun is pointed at the child?"

The boy's mother—he had heard the old woman call her Rina—sobbed, and clutched her son to her side. She sobbed, "No, *Herr* Major, *sie bitte*," she pleaded. "Please . . . please . . ."

"What will you do now, Madam?"

Anton was close enough now to hear and see what was happening. He nearly cried out when the sergeant roughly pushed his bubbe to the ground. He listened to the exchange carefully, but only really understood Bubbe, and her words frightened him. She was daring the major to execute her!

He watched in horror as the major answered her by pointing his pistol at David. Rina cried out, a horrible, aching sob, and begged for her son's life. Anton had to do something. If only he had a gun. *Think, Anton. You must get the soldiers away from Rina and Bubbe.* But how?

He shrugged his blanket bag off his shoulder. Inside he found the small hatchet Uncle Dmitri had given him to make tinder for the fires in the cave. That was the only weapon he had. One small hatchet against five armed men. It wouldn't do. He slammed his hand to the ground. *Ugh!* He'd hit something. That was just what he needed. To let another stone cause him pain.

But actually, that gave him an idea. He felt around on the ground until he had a handful of good-size stones.

He stood up and gauged the distance. He needed to get closer. Slowly, he moved toward the group until he was only thirty meters away. One of the soldiers— the sergeant, Anton thought—stood with his back to him. Taking careful aim, Anton chucked a rock with all his might. It flew through the air and struck the soldier between the shoulder blades, driving him to his knees.

"Was ist das?" the soldier shouted. The others raised their weapons and glanced about. But Anton was already on the move. As quietly as he could, he ran in an arc around the men, who were now yelling at one another in confusion. Taking careful aim, he hurled a second stone. This one struck one of the men in the thigh. He moved around the group again and threw a third. This time he missed. The stone skipped through the middle of the group.

The major ordered his men to shoot. Machine-gun fire spat in every direction. Anton dropped to the ground. The bullets whizzed over his head. When the firing stopped, he slowly stood and crept farther around the group. He chucked another rock. *Ping!* It hit one of the soldiers on the helmet, and the man staggered forward.

"Finden sie! Finden sie! Achtung!" the major shouted. *Find them!* The four soldiers took off running into the night while the major stayed behind to guard their prisoners.

Clutching the hatchet in his hand, Anton waited until the soldiers had disappeared. He circled slowly, quietly. When the major's back was to him, Anton crept forward out of the darkness. The cruel man who'd taken his bubbe turned, and his eyes went wide with surprise just as Anton brought the blunt side of the hatchet down on his head.

"Too bad gestapo officers don't wear helmets," Anton whispered as the blow hammered the major to his knees. A hand raised the Luger, but Anton swung again. This swipe did the trick. The major slumped forward, landing face-first on the ground.

"Bubbe, Rina," Anton said. "Come. We must hurry."

CHAPTER TWENTY

When Von Duesen came to, one of his men stood over him, splashing his face with water from a canteen. Eberhardt shone a flashlight in his eyes. Von Duesen touched his fingers to the sore spot on his crown and they came away bloody. His head ached.

"Where are the prisoners?" he demanded.

"Gone, *mein* major," Sergeant Eberhardt said.

"What? How could two women and a boy escape?" he said.

"We were attacked, *mein* major—"

Von Duesen pushed the canteen away and clambered to his feet. He felt woozy, but would not show weakness in front of his men. "We were not attacked, you fools!" He kicked a stone lying on the ground. "A boy threw rocks at us! They can't have gone far! Find them!"

"But which way, *mein* major?" Eberhardt asked.

"I don't care! It is an old woman, a mother, and a child!" He picked his Luger up off the ground. "Just find them!"

The four men split into teams of two and headed off into the black night, their flashlights working the ground as they searched the soil for any sign of tracks. They tried to cover as much ground as possible, but it was slow going. The potato fields were full of vines and made it difficult to find tracks.

"Beeilung! Ihr Idioten!" the major shouted. *Hurry, you idiots.* Von Duesen was despondent. How had everything gone so wrong? He could not return to headquarters empty-handed again.

He'd thought the partisan militia had attacked the half-track, but now he doubted that assumption. A militia patrol would consist of at least ten men. Wouldn't they have gunned the gestapo down to rescue the prisoners? But instead they had thrown rocks. Militias were sometimes short on supplies, of course. Could they have run out of ammunition? That didn't make sense. With ten men they would still have outnumbered his squad.

No, this was not a large group. And Von Duesen suspected it was personal. Someone could have followed them from the cave. If they were smart enough to tail the half-track, they might have been smart enough to sabotage it. And now they were attempting a rescue. He needed to find this mystery attacker.

If I return to headquarters with no prisoners, there will be consequences, Von Duesen thought. Karl knew he could be reassigned, demoted, or relieved of his command.

He could not allow that.

As the minutes passed, his men worked their way deeper and deeper into the fields. How could such feeble prisoners elude soldiers of the mighty gestapo? Von Duesen waited for an answer, his anger as complete as the silence of the night.

The quiet was shattered by the sound of machine-gun fire.

"Nein! Nein!" Von Duesen shouted as he ran toward his men. *"Nicht schiessen! Nicht schiessen!"* *Don't shoot.* If the prisoners were killed they could not be questioned. They would not be able to help him make the area *Judenfrei*.

His boots trampled the earth. The men were more than a hundred meters away. When Von Duesen arrived at their location his heart sank. Smoke still curled from the barrels of their guns. A flashlight illuminated the scene.

On the ground lay the mother and her child. Their bodies were riddled with bullet holes and blood seeped through their clothing.

"Spread out!" Major Von Duesen ordered. "We will not leave this place until we find whoever has attacked us!" He cracked his knuckles. "But take them alive. Do you hear me? Do not shoot them!"

Now more than ever he needed answers to his questions.

TWENTY-ONE

Anton did not know what to say. He and Bubbe watched the soldiers across the field arguing over the bodies of Rina and David.

Why had the gestapo fired their weapons? Surely, to interrogate their prisoners and find out where their friends and neighbors were hiding. He felt responsible. An enormous wave of guilt washed over him. He should have insisted Rina come with them. But she hadn't wanted to find the Priest's Grotto. She'd said she and David would be safer on their own. And now they were dead.

"Oh, Bubbe," Anton moaned. "What have I done? What have I done?"

Bubbe took his hand and squeezed it hard. "Anton, you did nothing wrong. Those men over there are pure evil. You have never seen it before. They have no conscience, no feeling, no remorse. You gave Rina and her son a chance. You did all you could do. Now you must pull yourself together. We will grieve for Rina and David later."

Anton knew she was right. But still, he felt a sadness he had never known before. It weighed on him as heavy as the boulders that had trapped him only days earlier. The only way he could wash away his grief was to focus on getting Bubbe to safety. But even then, he struggled to keep the guilt he felt at bay.

"I am sorry, Bubbe," Anton said.

"No, Anton, my child. It was God's will." Again, Bubbe spoke of God. Anton wondered how she could maintain her faith in such circumstances.

They walked on in silence. Each potato field they crossed looked the same to Anton. Time seemed to slow, the only marker the growling rumble of his belly. When they stopped to rest, Anton dropped to his knees and pulled a vine from the soil. Raw potatoes were chalky, but they were the only food around. He picked a dozen more and secreted them in his blanket. He and Bubbe would not go hungry. But they would need to find water soon.

"Bubbe?" he asked.

"Yes?"

"What do we do now? How do we find the Priest's Grotto?"

"We head north. Dmitri says the area is full of partisans. There are people there who have no love for the gestapo. If we can find them, they will help us find the caves where Dmitri and the others are headed."

"How far is it?"

"I do not know, Anton. I'm not even sure where we are now. Soon, daylight will come. Perhaps then we can determine where we are. But first we must find a place to hide."

Anton had no idea where that might be. In the starlight, all he could see were potato plants. Bubbe could not move quickly and it would be dawn soon. Already the eastern sky was growing lighter. If the major had indeed called reinforcements, soon the entire area would be crawling with gestapo.

Yet they had no choice but to keep walking. So they did, step after step in the soggy soil. Every bird that fluttered into the sky at their approach caused Anton's heart to thunder in his chest. He tried to will his grandmother to move faster, but he knew she was going as quickly as she could. Anton kept count, and every ten steps he looked behind him, studying the horizon and making sure that no one followed them.

After another hour, Anton spotted a copse of trees. Even better, there was a farmhouse, barn, and several small outbuildings on the other side of them.

"Bubbe, wait," Anton whispered. He gestured toward the farmhouse. It appeared deserted. With dawn approaching, someone should have been stirring inside. On a working farm, a lamp would be lit or a fire started before sunup. But the windows remained dark.

Even so, he tried to remain optimistic. "Perhaps the farmer can help us," he said.

Bubbe shook her head. "No, Anton. You must never approach someone you do not know. We are Jews. Many of our neighbors are not. They will turn us in to save themselves from the gestapo. We should keep going."

"Bubbe, please listen. I am tired. You are tired. We need to rest. If we cannot knock on the door of the house, perhaps we can sneak into the barn. There must be a hayloft. No one will know if we sleep there for an hour or two. Then when the sun comes up we can figure out where we must go next to find Uncle Dmitri. We can find places around the farm to hide until nightfall."

"I don't know, Anton," she said as she studied the house. Her shoulders slumped and she leaned heavily on her walking stick. He knew she was in pain, though she would die before she admitted it.

"Bubbe, we cannot continue after the sun comes up. These fields are too open. We need to hide. Besides, they have water," he said, pointing to a hand pump a few meters from the barn.

She studied her grandson. "When did you grow up, Anton?" she asked. "It was only yesterday you were toddling along behind your father, trying to do everything he did. Now you are almost a man."

Looking up at the barn, she smiled. "All right, we will do as you say. We will hide in the barn. Wait until darkness comes again. Then we will find your Uncle Dmitri."

Anton felt a tremendous sense of relief. Still, he was cautious. As they approached the barn, he kept the trees between them and the house. His instincts told him the house was deserted. Whoever lived there had packed up and left. But he wasn't sure enough to take a foolhardy risk. Anton kept his eyes on the house, with its neglected flower trellises and worn front steps, as they crept past it and headed for the barn.

Bubbe started for the door, but he gently took her elbow to stop her. He pointed to the pump. "Water first, Bubbe," he said. The pump held a tin cup on a hook. It was made of rusted iron, but looked to be in working order. The trouble was, a pump like this needed water poured down the shaft to prime it. And there was no water available to use.

Anton glanced around. If only there were a puddle or a rain barrel nearby. But he saw nothing. Then he spied a watering trough on the side of the barn. He removed the cup and headed around the corner to investigate. A centimeter of tepid water was a most welcome discovery! It would be enough. He scraped the cup along the bottom of the trough. Returning to the pump, he poured some of the water down the shaft and grasped the pump handle. He knew from experience the metal parts of the pump would squeak and groan when he lifted the handle. But if they wanted a drink, he had no other choice.

He pulled the handle upward and was rewarded with a loud shriek. To Anton it sounded as loud as a cannon shot. He poured more water down the pump shaft and the sound softened, but the pesky squeak would not go away. If there was anyone in the house it would surely alert them. Up and down he worked the handle, slowly priming the pump with the remaining water from the cup.

At first he thought the well might be dry, but then he heard a gurgling sound as water worked its way up the pipe and finally spilled out of the spigot. He pumped harder—he knew the water would be dirty and undrinkable at first. When it cleared, he rinsed out the cup, filled it to the brim, and handed it to Bubbe. She drank it dry in about three gulps. He filled it again and again she drank. Only when she was done did Anton take a turn. The water tasted earthy, but he didn't care. It was like heaven on his tongue. He had not realized how thirsty he was. He and Bubbe each drank another cup. All the time, he kept his eye on the house. Though he suspected it was empty, he couldn't help expecting the door to open or the windows to illuminate at any moment. But the house remained still.

When he and Bubbe finally entered the barn, he flipped on his flashlight. The room looked forgotten. An old tractor sat in front of a double door, but its tires had long gone flat. A hoe, a shovel, and a sickle hung on the wall. Very little else was left behind.

There were empty stalls where animals had once been kept. Now all that remained was a large pile of hay. The farmers had either turned their livestock loose or hitched them to a cart when they were leaving. Anton took the hoe from the wall and worked it through the hay, making sure it was free of rats and mice. Nothing scurried away.

"We can sleep here, Bubbe," he said. "If you are hungry, I have a few potatoes."

"No, Anton. I am too tired to eat, and right now that pile of hay looks like a wonderful, comfortable bed." She lay down on the hay, groaning in pain. She pulled her shawl around her shoulders and closed her eyes. A few moments later, she was softly snoring.

Anton went to the barn window and stared outside for a long time. If the Germans came, they'd never be able to run—not with Bubbe moving as slowly as she did. So he would have to be prepared. The door to the barn opened inward, but latched shut on the outside. He propped the hoe and shovel against it. If anyone pushed the door open, the clattering noise of the falling tools would wake him. Then he removed the sickle from the wall and checked the edge with his thumb. The blade was pocked with rust spots, but the edge was still sharp.

This will make a much better weapon than my little hatchet, he thought to himself as he lay down next to Bubbe.

Anton's eyelids felt heavy. Seconds later, he was asleep with the sickle's handle clutched tightly in his hand.

TWENTY-TWO

Major Von Duesen was livid. The sun had risen an hour ago, and he had been ordered to wait by the bodies of the dead woman and her child until General Steuben arrived. He understood that he had failed miserably. But the longer he waited, the farther away the old woman—and whoever had freed her—were getting, making them that much harder to catch.

He had been furious with his two privates for shooting down the *Juden*. They knew he wanted the fugitives captured alive. If General Steuben did not relieve him of his command for this debacle, Karl would make sure those two simpletons were reassigned. He would have them sent to the Russian front. But Karl had to admit that the world would not mourn the loss of two more Jews. If the woman was still alive, she and her child would have been sent away after her interrogation. They probably would have died anyway. Perhaps they had been spared future suffering. But really, that did not matter in the least. Their deaths were meaningless.

Headlights cut through the morning mist as three half-tracks and a truck carrying a platoon of soldiers turned off the road and rolled to a stop. The column was led by a staff car, decorated with a Nazi flag on either side of the hood flapping in the morning breeze. The sight of the car filled him with dread.

General Steuben did not wait for his driver to open his door for him, emerging from the Mercedes with grim purpose. If there was one thing Karl admired about his commanding officer, it was that General Steuben did not stand on ceremony or let the trappings of his rank get in the way of duty. He was a no-nonsense soldier who always got right down to business. And this morning, the business at hand meant explaining the absence of prisoners. Von Duesen suddenly wished he were anywhere but here.

The general's uniform was immaculate, his boots polished and gleaming. But he did not hesitate to walk into the muddy field where Von Duesen and his men stood near the bodies. Von Duesen and his men came to attention.

"Heil Hitler, *mein* general," he said.

The general repeated the salute. "Heil Hitler, Major." He did not look at Von Duesen. Instead, he studied the bodies lying in the field.

"Report," he ordered.

Von Duesen recounted the events of the previous evening. He told the general about tracking the two Jewish men to the cave, and the ambush that they'd executed. And how he had not yet been able to make radio contact with the lieutenant he had left in charge of rounding up the rest of the Jews who had been hiding in the cave's many tunnels. The older man's expression never changed.

"So you discovered a hiding place with many *Juden*. You left with three prisoners. Why did you not stay until the cave had been searched?" he demanded.

"The old woman, *mein* general," Von Duesen said. "She was obviously an important elder. A symbol and leader of the *Juden* in the cave. In truth, I thought of shooting her there. To break their spirit. But then I thought it wiser to remove her for interrogation. I believe she is giving the others instructions. A coded message of some kind. It seemed a better idea to remove her."

"I see," the general said. "And how did she escape?"

"We were attacked," he said.

The general's eyes narrowed. "Attacked? By who?"

"I do not know," Von Duesen replied. "At first I thought a partisan militia, but now I do not think so. They had no weapons and—"

"No weapons? Then how were you *'attacked'*?"

Major Von Duesen looked down. He found himself momentarily unable to speak.

Sergeant Eberhardt, perhaps hoping to save himself from a demotion, spoke up. "We were surrounded, *Herr* General," he responded with conviction. "And we were outnumbered. In the confusion, the prisoners escaped."

"I do not understand," Steuben huffed. "If partisans attacked you, why are you not dead? Why did they not gun you down and take your prisoners? Someone please explain this to me."

General Steuben's piercing blue eyes bored into Eberhardt. Karl had no great love for his sergeant. The man tried too hard to please. He didn't think. And he was no match for Steuben's pointed questioning. "We do not believe they were armed, *Herr* General," Von Duesen interjected.

"Excuse me?"

Von Duesen took a deep breath. He felt like his career with the gestapo was crashing right before him, here in the middle of a potato field in this god-forsaken country. The next words he spoke must be cautious.

"We know the militias are low on supplies. We believe they sabotaged our half-track, then when we were on foot, they hurled stones at us."

"I'm sorry?" The general raised his eyebrows. "I thought you said *stones*."

"That is correct, sir."

General Steuben said nothing. He clasped his hands behind his back and circled the bodies of the woman and her child. Von Duesen found it impossible to read his impassive face, even when the general completed his inspection and came to stand directly in front of Karl.

"Sergeant Eberhardt," General Steuben called.

"You and your squad will return to Borta, where you will file your reports and await my return."

The sergeant came to attention and saluted. "Heil Hitler," he said. Turning, he ordered his men toward one of the half-tracks. *"Mach schnell! Mach schnell!"* he said. The men marched away from the two officers in double time.

The general was quiet for a moment.

"What to do with you, Major? What to do with you . . ." the general muttered.

"Sir . . ."

The general held up a gloved hand. "I do not need to tell you that you have made innumerable mistakes in the last several days. I'm sure someone of your intelligence and ability understands that."

Von Duesen sensed it would be best to remain silent.

"If the *Juden* hear that an old woman has eluded you, it will raise their spirits. We must get our hands on her. And you will lead the search. You will find this woman and bring her to Borta. If you do not . . ." the general's words trailed off.

"Thank you, *mein* general," Von Duesen said. He could not believe his luck. It was still possible for him to salvage this mess and restore the general's fine opinion of him.

The general turned on his heel and headed toward his car. Von Duesen followed sheepishly behind. As he walked he thought about the "attack." His hand went to the swollen spot on his head, where he had been clubbed to the ground. He had barely seen the face of his attacker, but he could have sworn it belonged to a child. No, he did not think a militia had attacked them. It was a single person, two at most. That boy and perhaps another. His fury grew as he pondered how they had outwitted him.

They had made an enemy last night.

One they would regret.

CHAPTER TWENTY-THREE

In his sleepy stupor, Anton thought the far-off buzzing that roused him was an insect. He sneezed as he sat up in his makeshift bed. Hay stuck to his clothing and his face. Dust tickled his nose. A few hours of sleep had not erased the exhaustion in his bones.

The buzzing grew louder. As he came fully awake, he realized it was not the sound of insects, but engines.

Anton leapt to his feet, ran to the barn door, and moved the hoe and shovel aside. Then, cracking the door open, he peered outside. A fingernail of sun had just cleared the horizon in the east, but the dawn light was not yet bright enough to see anything. The engines—and there had to be many of them—rumbled from the south. Anton recognized the grinding of the half-tracks. That could mean only one thing. The gestapo was coming.

He raced back to the hay pile where Bubbe still slept. He knew she was drained and he wished he could let her sleep longer, but he did not think that would be wise.

"Bubbe! Bubbe!" He shook her gently by the shoulder. She awoke with a start.

"What is it, my child?" Unlike Anton, she was instantly alert.

"The gestapo. Coming up the road. We need to hide."

Bubbe struggled to her feet. She shook the hay from her hair and clutched her walking stick.

"How much time do we have?"

"Very little," Anton said. "I couldn't see the half-tracks, but I could hear them coming."

"If only we could reach the forest before they arrive," she said.

Anton shook his head. "We don't have time. We're going to have to find a place to hide here." He glanced up at the loft. There was a ladder on the far wall. "Can you climb, Bubbe?"

"I can try," she said.

She hurried her tired body to the ladder. He heard her groan in pain as she raised her left foot and placed it on the first rung. Next, she tried to pull herself up. From the sharp intake of breath, Anton knew that he had asked the impossible. They would never make it to the loft in time.

What will we do? Anton's eyes darted around the barn. When they settled on the hay pile, he realized there was one task that could not wait.

"Bubbe, help me, please!" he called as he raked the hay back and forth. They needed to remove the outlines their bodies had made when they slept. Bubbe used her walking stick to stir the hay, making it look as natural as possible. As they worked, Anton struggled to think of a place they could hide. Uncle Dmitri had thought the cave perfect because it kept them safe even though they were right beneath the gestapo's feet.

That's it! Anton thought. Trust Uncle Dmitri to inspire an idea that might actually work.

"Come, Bubbe!" he said. "We must hurry."

"Where will we hide, my child?"

"Trust me," he said, taking her by the arm. "There is no time to lose."

They scurried into the spot Anton had thought of, moments before a Mercedes led three gestapo half-tracks and a troop truck into the yard.

"Spread out," a familiar voice shouted. "Find them. *Schnell, schnell!*"

The soldiers leapt from the back of the truck and the half-tracks. Several of them took the barn. The rest spread out over the grounds. All of them carried submachine guns.

Six of the men strode toward the house. A small staircase led to the front door. Before even checking to see if it was locked, they kicked it open with a *crash*.

It's a good thing the people who lived here have cleared out, thought Anton. Watching the gestapo break into their home would have been terrifying.

If he and Bubbe were going to survive, they needed to endure the next few minutes. It appeared the major was determined to leave no part of the farm unsearched. The soldiers disappeared into the house, their boots thundering across the wooden floors.

Anton could hear them shout, *"Klar! Klar!"* as they cleared each room.

Bubbe sat with her eyes closed, squeezing his hand so tightly he thought she might crush his fingers. She whispered prayers, and though her voice didn't carry much, Anton wished he could convince her to be silent. He knew that in this moment of peril, Bubbe needed to speak to God. Her faith strengthened her will to fight. But Anton was not convinced that prayers alone would save them from the guns of the gestapo. Rina had been devout, and her prayers had gone unanswered.

When the soldiers entered the barn, Anton's pulse thudded at his temples. The men searched the loft and the stalls. Cold morning air blew through the wide open doorway and swirled pieces of hay around their legs. Two of the soldiers had rifles with bayonets attached to the barrels. The major gave a command and the two men advanced on the pile of straw. Their bayonets gleamed.

Anton held his breath.

CHAPTER TWENTY-FOUR

Major Von Duesen was frustrated. His men had searched the area for the last few hours, looking behind every rock, inspecting every ditch and the branches of every tree. And now as they searched this farm, it looked like once again they would come up short. He would come up short. That would not do.

Ransacking the barn was proving fruitless. The old woman was not in the hayloft or hidden under the tractor. But there was still one place left to investigate, one last hope for vindication. A large pile of hay in the stall. It was more than big enough to hide two or even three people.

"Lieutenant Hinkel," Von Duesen said. "Have your squad fix bayonets." He pointed to the pile of hay, and the lieutenant understood immediately. As he barked a command, two privates removed their bayonets from their belts and attached them to their rifle barrels. They strode quietly to the hay pile. The major held up his hand.

"If you are hiding now and surrender," he said in a loud voice, "I promise you will not be harmed. If you do not, well, my men will begin stabbing the hay pile at random. You have ten seconds to comply."

As the major counted, time seemed to slow down. His voice was impossibly loud. "*Eins, Zwei, Drei . . .*" he said, giving himself a second between each number. The two privates stood poised to strike at his command.

"Your last chance," Von Duesen warned. From the corner of his eye, he saw a slight frown cross the lieutenant's face. As if his hesitancy was a sign of weakness. He had no doubt Hinkel would report this moment to the general when they returned to headquarters.

When he reached ten, he nodded and the two men drove their bayonets into the hay, once, twice, three times. But all they struck was the dirt below.

"*Halten,*" he said. The men stopped. The major walked into the stall and kicked the hay out onto the barn floor. He cursed as he stomped his way through the pile of hay. When he had emptied the stall, he punched the wooden wall in frustration. It was empty. The pile of hay hid nothing. Another waste of time.

If anyone had been there, they were long gone by now.

CHAPTER TWENTY-FIVE

"Anton, are we safe?" Bubbe whispered.

The German soldiers had returned to the troop truck and the half-tracks. The roar of the engines was deafening as they rolled out of the yard.

"Not yet, Bubbe," Anton said. The gestapo was famous for faking a departure and then abruptly doubling back or leaving a few hidden soldiers behind to surprise and capture anyone whom they had not been able to find in their search.

Anton knew that Bubbe was uncomfortable, but only his quick thinking had managed to save them so far. He would not let his efforts be undone by impatience.

"Just a little longer, Bubbe," he said. "I promise."

She nodded her head in agreement. Anton studied her tired, wrinkled face. Just enough light crept into their hiding place that he could see the fierce determination in her eyes. He remembered her standing in front of the gestapo major in the cave. How she had refused to allow him to gain the upper hand, or to intimidate her. It was impossible to know how many lives her stubborn willpower had saved.

And now the survival of his family depended on keeping her alive. Dmitri and Pavel were fine men. Good uncles who had done their best to teach him, raise him, and keep him from thinking too much about his father's fate. But even they were not made of steel like Bubbe. She was the rock of the family. And if she did not live through this crisis, then neither would they. Though of course, Anton could not be sure that Pavel was alive now. But he did know that Bubbe was the glue holding them together. And the responsibility of reuniting her with the family was his now. He could not fail.

"I think it is safe now," Anton said after a few very long minutes. He removed the trellis from the side of the small set of steps leading to the front door of the farmhouse. They had hidden there, huddled in the shadows while the soldiers had ransacked the house and the barn. He'd taken a gamble that the search party would be so preoccupied with the obvious hiding places, they would not think to look beneath the stairs. He and Bubbe had barely had enough time to make it from the barn, pull the trellis free, and replace it behind them before the vehicles arrived. Anton was glad the gestapo did not have dogs with them, or he and Bubbe would surely have been discovered.

Anton helped his grandmother lumber from the small, dark space and winced at the guttural groan that slipped from her lips as she straightened up.

He was torn about what they should do next. On one hand, the gestapo had already searched the farm and found nothing. It was unlikely they would return. Earlier, he had seen smoke rising on the horizon and assumed they were burning the buildings they had searched so they wouldn't have to examine them again. But they had not burned this one. Perhaps the major was so angry he had forgotten to give the order. If that was the case, he and Bubbe might remain on the farm in relative comfort while they figured out what to do next.

But on the other hand, the longer they remained in one spot, the more likely it was that someone would discover them.

Still, Bubbe needed rest, and Anton thought he might look for supplies they could use.

"Come, Bubbe," he said, taking her hand and leading her up the stairs.

"What are we doing?"

"We are going to wait here until nightfall. We will rest. Perhaps sleep on a real bed."

"Are you sure, Anton? What if the gestapo return?"

He led her to a bedroom off the kitchen. The bed looked like a cloud from heaven. Anton helped his grandmother sit down and smiled when he saw the worry on her face disappear, even if only for the moment.

"Do not worry, Bubbe," Anton said. "I will keep watch. If the gestapo return, we will hide as we did before. They will not find us. When it is dark and you are rested, we will head north to the rendezvous point and find the others. The Germans will not find us. God has made us invisible, Bubbe! He has made us undetectable in the night. The darkness will protect us. You need not worry. Rest, Bubbe. We have a long journey ahead of us this evening."

As his grandmother looked up at him, he saw tears in her eyes.

"Bubbe!" he said. "Is something wrong? Are you ill?"

"No. I am not sick. It's just that you remind me so much of your father," she said as she brought her hand to his face. "You are a good boy, Anton. Brave and strong, like your papa. Soon, you will be a man. I am very proud of you."

Anton felt that his chest might burst with pride. He smiled at her. "Come," he said, helping her into bed. "You rest. I will keep watch."

"Thank you, my child." She closed her eyes while he pulled a quilt over her.

He left the bedroom and walked the first floor of the house, glancing out each window. For a moment he considered venturing outside to find some wood to build a fire in the stove. He still had the potatoes. With a little boiling water he could fix a feast. But the smoke would be visible for kilometers. No, when Bubbe woke up they would eat the potatoes raw. It was better than nothing. He would not lose his grand-mother for something so careless.

He checked the windows again. There was no sign of life on the road in either direction. Then he began opening the cupboards and closets. They may not have had a feast, but that did not mean they could not find a treasure left behind. As he searched he remembered the touch of Bubbe's hand on his face.

He would not let her down.

Not ever.

TWENTY-SIX

Major Von Duesen stood at attention in front of General Steuben's desk. The general was taking his time reviewing the report Karl had made. Steuben was clearly happy to let him stew in his own juices.

It was nearly impossible for Karl to contain his anger. To think he had been outwitted by an old woman and her protectors. It left him furious. At least he could claim the deaths of the young woman and her child. He and his men had rid the world of two useless Jews. The area was two bodies closer to becoming *Judenfrei*. And he had exposed their hiding place, which they could no longer use as a safe haven. That had to count for something. But allowing the old woman to escape had cast all of his accomplishments in a negative light.

When he first entered headquarters—the Borta courthouse that the gestapo had taken over—he saw a few of his fellow officers smile and turn away, trying to hide their laughter. Word of his failure had spread quickly. He marched toward the general's office. He was on his way to the door when the voice of a man he'd known his entire career forced him to turn around.

"Major Von Duesen," Colonel Mehringer called out. "I have a mission for you."

Karl stopped and saluted the colonel, who continued. "There is a convent nearby that needs to be guarded. General Steuben would like to know if you would need two or three battalions to make sure they do not escape."

All the officers broke out into laughter. Von Duesen tried to maintain a good-natured smile, but inside he burned with resentment. He took note of who was laughing. He would get them. He would get them all.

They could think him a fool, but Karl was cunning. He would undoubtedly be reassigned as punishment for his failure. He'd be stuck overseeing a supply station or prisoner transport, or some other tedious duty. That was fine. Let them think he was humiliated. He would take the assignment without complaint, but he would find a way to use it to his advantage. He would look for any information on the *Juden* who'd escaped that unlucky cave. If they had not yet been caught, they must have another hiding place. He would find it. That would redeem him in the eyes of his commanding officer. He had focused on that goal as he turned away from the laughter and approached whatever fate awaited him in Steuben's office.

The general had finally finished with the report and placed it on the desk in front of him. He straightened the papers and tidied his pens, anything to make Von Duesen wait. It was infuriating, but Karl kept his face as still as if it had been carved from stone. No matter what happened, he would show no emotion.

"Do you have anything to say, Major?"

"*Nein, mein* general. Everything is in my report."

"You still believe you were attacked by partisans?"

"Yes, *mein* general. Now more than ever," Von Duesen said.

The general leaned back in his chair and studied him.

"Why?"

"Intelligence reports," Von Duesen replied.

"Explain."

"I have read the reports from our infantry units in the field as well as the after-action bulletins from SS interrogations, as I am sure you have. We know the militias in this area are short of supplies, low on ammunition, food, everything. So why would they risk an attack on an armed gestapo squad if they had no ammunition?"

"Why?"

"Because the old woman was . . . is . . . important."

"What? How could a woman who can barely walk be important? She is just a Jew!"

"I do not know specifically, *mein* general. But think of it. What if she leads the resistance? Or perhaps she guides the *Juden* to safety. She could know the locations of all of their safe houses. Of course, she might be nothing more than a symbol. But whatever she is, she was too important to be captured."

The general steepled his fingers, his face a mask of concentration. For a moment, Von Duesen thought he had been convincing. If Steuben would just give him another chance, he would find the woman and give her what she deserved. And the boy who'd blud-geoned him, too.

"*Nein*," the general said, sitting up in his chair. "I do not see this woman as anything other than a hapless Jew hiding in cave. No one who is trying to survive would place their fates in the hands of an old woman."

Von Duesen's heart sank, but he would not let his disappointment show. Somehow he would find a way to get what he wanted. Revenge.

"You are being reassigned to prisoner transport. A truck full of prisoners waits outside. It is fueled and ready to depart. That is all, *Herr* Major."

Von Duesen came to attention and saluted. "Heil Hitler," he said. He turned smartly on his heel and left the general's office. Making his way through head-quarters, he exhaled. His worst fears had been realized. Prisoner transport—an assignment that gave him no way to shine. As the general had promised a truck was waiting by the courthouse steps, its engine running.

A ragged and motley group of *Juden* had been stuffed into the truck bed. Exhaustion lined their faces.

They were mostly women, children, and old men. The driver—a sergeant—saluted Major Von Duesen as he climbed into the passenger seat of the cab.

It would be dark soon. Karl waited patiently as the truck lurched into gear.

He had a plan. And darkness would be the perfect time to execute it.

TWENTY-SEVEN

When Bubbe finally woke, the sky was dark. Anton's inventory of the house had revealed almost nothing of any use. He'd found a small container of salt, two empty jars he had filled with water from the pump, and a butter knife. They would take all of it, along with the quilt.

They dined on raw potatoes and water. Bubbe looked better after resting, but Anton knew she would still need to move slowly as they tried to find the others. Traveling at night would slow them even more.

"Bubbe, where is this Priest's Grotto? Where are we to meet Uncle Dmitri?" Anton asked.

"It is nearly five kilometers north of where we were. We have a long walk ahead of us. We may not make it before morning. If that is the case, we will have to find another place to hide."

Anton considered this while he chewed. He hoped

they could reunite with the remaining members of their group, but he was worried about locating the rendezvous point. If he and Bubbe lost their way, they would need to follow the river . . . and that was how the gestapo had discovered them in the first place. He hoped it would not come to that.

"Anton, there is something we need to discuss," Bubbe said.

"What is it?"

"It is about what happened in the field with the gestapo. What you did to rescue me. You must not do such a thing again."

"What? Bubbe—"

She held up her hand. When Bubbe was serious, a look came over her face that Anton recognized. It was stern, but not angry. It meant he was to obey her every word. He had seen it many times.

"I am grateful that you saved my life, Anton. I know that you love me and you were very brave. But you must never do such a thing again. You could have . . ." Her voice broke off as her eyes filled with tears. "You could have been killed. You are so much like your father. Smart. Dutiful. Courageous. You remind me of him more and more every day. But I cannot lose you, too."

"But Bubbe, you have not lost Papa! He is in the west, fighting with the Polish army. We do not know his fate. He could return to us when the war is over!"

"True. But war is chaos. We do not know if he is alive or dead. The militias have stolen Pavel from me. Soon, they or the Russian army will come to claim Dmitri for their ranks. And if this war lasts long enough, it will take you, too. When you are older—when you are a man—you will decide if you will fight. You and you alone. But for now, you will stay alive. And if I am captured again, you will not take foolish chances. Your priority is *your* life and safety, *not* mine. I need you to swear to me."

Anton wanted to protest, but he knew Bubbe would insist. They could argue for hours and her position would not change. He would do his best to stay alive and prevent her from being captured again. And he would give her the words she wanted. He just did not know whether he could stand by them.

"I swear, Bubbe," he said. "I will not take such a foolish chance again."

Bubbe patted him on the hand. "You are a good boy, Anton. Your mother and your father would be so proud."

She stood up and stretched. "We should get moving. We have far to go, and we do not know when another gestapo patrol might pass by without warning. We will be safer once we reach the forest.

Anton was not sure he agreed, but he gathered up their supplies. He packed the water jars carefully in the blanket pack. He hooked it over his shoulder, then he and Bubbe ventured into the darkness.

The only way they could find the Priest's Grotto was to backtrack until they recognized a landmark well enough to know which direction they should head next. Soon, the farmhouse was behind them. They crossed the rough terrain of the field and eventually were enveloped in the hardwood forest. With very little light, it was slow going. They had to navigate the forest floor while watching out for tree roots and low-hanging branches.

After about an hour, they stopped to rest. Bubbe was breathing hard, so Anton gave her a sip of water.

But they could not dally for long. Bubbe insisted that they plow ahead.

A bit farther on they came to the river and Anton finally recognized where they were. In fact, they were close to their original hiding place. He'd known they needed to find a familiar place to orient themselves, but walking along the river was exactly the thing he had been hoping to avoid.

Anton stopped and listened.

"What is it?" Bubbe whispered.

"This is the river where Uncle Dmitri and the other men gathered our water. I believe the gestapo used it to track us to the cave."

"So you think they may have planted men nearby to catch us returning to our hiding spot?"

"Yes, Bubbe," he said. "To be safe, we should cross to the other side of the river. We must travel as quietly as possible. If they were smart, they would hide on this side of the river, closest to the cave entrance. But in truth, it is impossible to know what is in their heads."

"But crossing the river is not safe," Bubbe said.

"It will be if we find the right spot," Anton replied. "Lend me your walking stick."

Anton took the offered staff and found a flat spot on the bank. He poked ahead of him with the walking stick, feeling along the bottom of river. Soon, he stood in the water up to his knees. The bottom of the river was rocky, not muddy, which would make it easier to cross. He kept creeping forward until the water reached his waist. But with a few more steps he had crossed to the other side.

He retraced his steps and took Bubbe by the arm. As they entered the water, she winced at how cold it was. But Anton held her tightly, using the staff to keep them upright. The current was not strong and they slowly worked their way to the other side. Anton removed his coat and shirt and wrung them out. Bubbe bunched up her skirt, twisting it in her hands to do the same.

"We must be quiet, Bubbe," he said. "If the gestapo is here, they will be watching the river. We will go around to the west and then circle back."

Before he could say another word, someone grabbed him from behind and a hand closed over his mouth.

TWENTY-EIGHT

Sergeant Weigert, who drove the truck, was an unrelenting talker. Despite Von Duesen's gruff one-word answers, Weigert droned on and on. Even when Karl did not answer him at all, he was not deterred. Within a few kilometers, Karl swore he knew the man's entire life history. How Weigert was born in Dresden, but grew up in Düsseldorf. His father was an engineer and his mother had died when he was sixteen. He dropped out of college to join the army and on and on and on.

Von Duesen had no interest in any of his yammering. He was looking for the right spot to implement his plan. So far nothing had proved suitable. But he knew the territory well from rounding up *Juden*. Soon, they would arrive at a place that would work perfectly. *This truck would be better used for hunting than transporting*, he thought to himself.

Though he appeared calm and collected on the outside, inside he still seethed at the treatment he'd received from General Steuben. Yes, he had lost his prisoners. His men had gunned down the woman and child. But it was a single unfortunate mistake. He and his squad had captured more Jews than any other in the entire regiment. He was a genius at sniffing out their hiding places and imprisoning them. But all that had been undone by one single error.

On they drove, the sergeant yammering away. Von Duesen was not sure whether Weigert even realized that his passenger had stopped participating in the conversation. Karl occupied himself by looking out the windshield at the passing countryside, waiting for the right spot to appear.

Finally, after several more kilometers, he saw it. The road bisected two large wheat fields and was lined by irrigation ditches on either side. There were no houses or villages around for kilometers.

"*Halten*," he ordered.

"*Mein* major?"

"*Halten Sie*," Von Duesen repeated.

"*Mein* major, our orders—"

"I was given new orders before we left," he said. He pulled several sheets of folded paper from inside the coat pocket of his uniform. In reality, they were not official documents of any kind—but the sergeant did not know that.

"*Ja, mein* major," he said. With a shrug he applied the brakes and the large truck came to a lumbering stop in the middle of the road.

"Now what, *mein* major?"

"Go to the rear of the truck, open the tailgate, and order the *Juden* out. Have them line up in front of the ditch."

"Major?" Weigert was clearly confused by his request.

"Do it. *Schnell, schnell.*"

Sensing something in his superior's voice, Weigert hurriedly opened the door and scrambled out. A few seconds later, Von Duesen heard the sergeant bark an order in Ukrainian. Even though it was a large truck, he felt it bounce as the Jews climbed out. He took a deep breath. Now was the time. Sergeant Weigert's machine gun lay on the seat next to him. He grabbed it, along with two extra clips of ammunition, and exited the vehicle.

In the darkness he could see the silhouettes of the prisoners milling about in the middle of the road. Weigert was trying to herd them in front of the irrigation canal, but they ignored him.

"All of you, line up in front of the ditch," Von Duesen commanded in his loudest, most serious tone. He did not speak Ukrainian, and had to repeat himself twice, but eventually they quietly did as he ordered.

These Jews had no fight left in them. For months they had been hunted, beaten, tortured, starved, and imprisoned. Now they were resigned to their fates. Von Duesen stalked to the middle of the line.

"Turn and face the field," he shouted. What could they do, but comply?

A few of the prisoners began to pray. When all of them had turned, Von Duesen racked the slide on the machine gun and pulled the trigger. The gun jumped in his hands as bullets leapt from the barrel. The noise was deafening.

Lead ripped into the bodies before him. The children went down first, tumbling into the ditch. A few of the younger women tried to run, but they did not get far. When one of the old men tried to turn as if to fight, the bullets knocked him backward, and he fell screaming into the trench.

Von Duesen walked to the edge and peered in at the bodies. A few of them still moved. He inserted a fresh clip into the gun and fired at the bodies again. When the clip emptied and the bullets were gone and the night was silent again, finally it was done. He had not relished the task, but he needed the truck to find that old woman and save his career. This was the only way.

He turned to find Sergeant Weigert staring at him in disbelief.

"*Mein Gott, Herr* Major," he said. "*Was haben Sie getan?*" *What have you done?*

Von Duesen looked directly into the sergeant's eyes. He wanted to make sure the man understood him.

"I have done, Sergeant, what needed to be done." He turned toward the truck. "Come," he said. "We have a long drive ahead of us."

CHAPTER TWENTY-NINE

The hand covering Anton's mouth smelled like dirt. It was all he could think of. Bubbe let out a gasp as another hand snaked out of the darkness and enveloped her mouth as well. Anton had been so careful. How had the gestapo found them?

He fumbled at the blanket pack around his shoulder. The small hatchet he carried was secreted there. If he could get it out, they might stand a chance of getting away. It had worked once before, after all. He thrashed and squirmed, trying desperately to free himself. Close by, he saw his grandmother doing the same. She whacked at her assailant with her walking stick and he could hear her muffled cries as she fought.

"Hold still," the voice behind him said. "Anton, hold still."

It took him a moment to realize that whoever held him knew his name. And then a moment longer to notice that the voice was speaking in Yiddish. How could this be? A gestapo soldier would speak German or maybe Ukrainian. *It must be a trick*, he thought as he struggled harder to free himself.

"Anton, Anton, stop," the voice said. "It is me! Your uncle Dmitri."

Uncle Dmitri? Here? How?

Anton could not believe it. Somehow, the Germans had captured his friends and neighbors and tortured them into revealing the group's secrets. Anton twisted his head back and forth until he worked his mouth free, then bit down hard on the hand covering him.

"Ow!" The voice behind him muttered, trying desperately to keep quiet. "Anton, it is me. Stop it!" The man released him, and when Anton turned around, to his shock, he found his uncle Dmitri standing in front of him, his face lit by moonlight. Another man he recognized from the cave, Herman, released his grandmother. Dmitri shook his bitten hand, trying to make the pain go away.

"When did you learn to bite like a mule?" he asked.

"Uncle Dmitri," Anton said. "What are you doing here?" Before he could get an answer, his grandmother crossed the distance between them and threw her arms around her son.

"Dmitri! Oh, my precious son. I thought I would never see you again." She cried tears of joy, her small, bony shoulders shaking as Dmitri held her. He stroked her head.

"*Muter. Muter,*" he said softly. *Mother. Mother.*

"How did you find us?" Anton asked.

"We've been keeping watch," Herman said. "The gestapo has been through the area almost every night looking for stragglers. We have been waiting until the Germans are not watching, and gathering up those who do not know the way to the Priest's Grotto."

"Yes," Dmitri said. "Sixteen of our original group is already there, plus three other families that we found running from the gestapo. The rest . . . well, we have no way of knowing what has become of them."

Bubbe told Dmitri what had happened to them. When she told him the fate of Rina and David, Dmitri grabbed her hand and together they bowed their heads in prayer. When they finished, Dmitri placed his hand on his nephew's shoulder.

"You did well, Anton," he said. "I owe you thanks for saving my mother. But she is right—you cannot take such a foolish chance in the future. You are brave, but bravery alone will not keep you alive. I think God smiles on you, for you were also lucky. The gestapo is cunning. Word will get out about what you have done. They will not be so careless the next time."

"I understand, Uncle. It's just . . . I couldn't let them take Bubbe away without doing something. It felt as if the hand of God was guiding me. With Papa gone . . ." His words trailed off.

"I know, lad. I know." Dmitri squeezed his shoulder. "We have had much taken from us. Yet here we are, alive. And it is God's wish that we stay that way. You must remember that always."

"I will, Uncle. I promise."

"Is everyone healthy? Safe?" Bubbe asked.

"Yes, Mother," Dmitri said. "And there is someone waiting for you who you will very much want to see.

Pavel is with us. He got separated from his partisan militia when we found him. His short time with them was most productive. He has become very resourceful. But there will be time to discuss all of that later. Now we must make haste."

They started off through the woods, following the riverbank. The night was cool, but sweat soon flowed down Anton's back and forehead as they took up a quick pace. Behind him, he could hear Bubbe breathing hard.

"Uncle," he said. "Bubbe needs help. She cannot keep up."

From behind, Bubbe whacked him on the hip with her walking stick. "Grandsons should learn to tend their own pasture. I am fine," she said.

"No, *Muter*. Anton is right. Herman and I will find a way to carry you. Now you must rest." He removed a canteen from his belt. "Stay here and drink. We will return shortly." Anton took the canteen, and then Dmitri and Herman disappeared into the darkness.

"Dmitri! Where are you going?" Bubbe whispered. She received no answer. Anton could hear the men moving off into the darkness. Anton led Bubbe to a fallen tree that she could sit on. He gave her the canteen and she drank from it greedily.

Sometimes, Anton marveled at how strong she was. Bubbe had raised her three boys, then taken over raising Anton when his mother had died. She worked the fields, tended the garden, helped with harvest, cooked their meals, and kept the house. When Papa had left to join the Polish army, she had taken on his share of the chores as well. And all of that had taken its toll. Though she would be loath to admit it, Bubbe was growing old. But still she had the heart of a warrior.

He remembered how she'd stood up to the gestapo in the cave. How fiercely she had stood. How proudly. She had bought time for the rest of the group, a collection of ragged strangers she adopted as her family. He remembered the look in the major's eyes. The force of her will had taken him aback. It was inconceivable to him that an old woman was not afraid of him or his soldiers or his guns.

It was the major who had been afraid. Later, when Bubbe told him that Germany was losing the war, Anton had seen his fear again.

Is Bubbe right? he thought. *Is that why the major was so scared? Could this long and deadly war truly be coming to an end? And does that mean I might finally learn what has become of Papa?*

His thoughts were interrupted by the return of his uncle and Herman. They carried two saplings with a cloth blanket wrapped around them—a makeshift stretcher.

"Hop aboard," Dmitri told his mother.

"I will not," Bubbe said.

"Mother, there is no time," Dmitri said.

"I am fully capable of walking," she insisted.

"Bubbe," Anton said. "Please. Uncle Dmitri is right. We have a great distance to travel. We cannot delay. It will be daylight soon. For so long you have carried us, Bubbe. Let us carry you."

Bubbe put her hands on Anton's cheeks. She brushed back the hair from his forehead and smiled.

"Your father was always able to talk me into things I did not wish to do. But I will not put all of you in danger. Help your bubbe into this contraption. And tell your uncle if he drops me, he will regret it. He is not too big to spank."

"The uncle is standing right here," Dmitri said, chuckling.

"Yes, you are, but you never listen. Anton is a good boy. He pays attention."

Herman and Dmitri held the stretcher at each end and Anton helped Bubbe settle into it. The men carried her through the trees, and though it was harder to navigate with the long stretcher, they were making much better time. After a while, Anton glanced down at Bubbe to find that she had gone to sleep.

The sky was beginning to lighten in the east.

"How much further, Uncle Dmitri?" Anton asked.

"Another kilometer, but we will have to cross the river again," he said.

Dmitri had already found a shallow spot. He and Herman carried Bubbe across the river without her waking. Anton followed along and soon they were on the other side.

Before long, the trees thinned out. They came to a grassy meadow. There was a large circular depression in the middle of it that reminded Anton of the cave they had hidden in. Herman and Dmitri carried Bubbe to an area in the center where three large boulders thrust up out of the ground.

"*Muter*," Dmitri whispered. "We are here."

She awoke slowly, and Anton helped her off the stretcher. "Already?" she asked.

"Yes, *Muter*. This is it. The Priest's Grotto. Come, the entrance is well hidden." Herman tossed the saplings aside and gathered up the blanket. Dmitri led them to a spot between the three boulders. He pulled back a small hatch that had been covered with twigs and branches for camouflage. He lifted the hatch and flipped on his flashlight. They made their way down a gently sloping passageway until the slope steepened and they had to take hold of a rope that had been strung along the tunnel to keep their footing. A few meters later, the ground leveled out again and opened into a large chamber. The Priest's Grotto was far bigger than the previous cave they had lived in. Inside they were reunited with old friends and met the new families. They had created a kitchen space, and some areas had been made into sleeping quarters.

"One of the tunnels leads to an underground lake," Dmitri said, pointing to a passageway. "There is plenty of fresh water. No need to risk going out at night to gather it. If we can build up our food stores, we will scarcely need to venture outside at all."

Anton looked around and took it all in. They had survived. His family felt almost whole again. And for now, this would be their home.

EIGHTEEN MONTHS LATER

CHAPTER THIRTY

Captain Karl Von Duesen sat at his desk at gestapo headquarters in Borta as a clerk dropped another stack of intelligence reports in front of him. He sighed. He took the top folder off the pile, opened it, and started reading. It was a boring, poorly written after-action report of a skirmish between an SS armored column and a partisan militia. There was nothing useful in it. He stamped it as "read," signed his initials, and closed the folder, placing it on the to-be-filed stack.

His grand plan had backfired. When he killed the prisoners he was supposed to be transporting and commandeered the truck, he'd thought he'd found a way to fix all his problems. If he could just recover the *Juden* he'd lost, General Steuben would see his ambition and tenacity and be impressed. But he'd scoured the countryside for weeks looking for the fugitives, and had not found them. When he returned he was demoted to captain, given three months in the brig, and after his release, assigned a desk job. He hated it.

General Steuben had informed him that he was lucky to have avoided a court-martial. Von Duesen could not fathom the logic of it. He had simply executed Jews, something the Nazis did all the time with impunity. These were not important people. They were not military prisoners who could reveal strategic information. They were barely more than animals. He had saved the Reich the time and money it would have taken to provide care for them.

But gestapo leadership did not view it that way. General Steuben had berated him for the damage he had done to the Nazi cause. When word of such incidents got out, the German cause suffered. Collaborators became less trusting of the gestapo, and sometimes stopped cooperating. And it became more difficult to reach the führer's goal of making Ukraine *Judenfrei*. Once the Russians and Americans were defeated, Ukraine would become an important agricultural center for the new Reich. It would be the breadbasket of the Aryan nation. When German families and farmers were moved into the formerly Ukrainian territory, the cooperation of the people would be essential for a peaceful transition. Von Duesen's actions had made such cooperation much more difficult.

But Karl cared for none of that. For the last year and half he had used his newly assigned duties to search for the old woman who had caused his professional demise. He had spent countless off-duty hours combing the countryside, looking for any sign of the two of them or any group they might have traveled with. In truth, he did not have much to go on. The description he gave to the villagers and farmers he met was vague. An old woman dressed like a peasant, using a walking stick. A young boy about twelve years old, his face covered in mud and grime, also dressed like a peasant. It fit the description of hundreds of people in the surrounding area.

He had even gone to the old cave where the *Juden* had first been captured. He had combed every nook and cranny of it himself. It had taken hours and hours. He hoped they might have left behind some clue to where they would go next. Perhaps a note or a hand-drawn map. But his search had proved fruitless. There was nothing left in the cave but a few cooking utensils, articles of clothing, and children's playthings.

Now he was stuck. And the worst part of it was, as much as he hated—refused—to believe it, the war was not going well for the Reich. Italy was lost. The cowardly Italian army and government had folded like a cheap tent the moment the Americans showed up on their soil. They had surrendered and left the heavy fighting to the German troops. Yet the führer had no choice but to try to force them back—he could not allow an attack on Germany from the south.

And somehow, despite the fierce resistance of the Reich's finest soldiers, the Americans had invaded Western Europe. Landing on the beaches of France, they were now pushing the Reich back to the homeland. They had already retaken Paris, forcing the mighty German army to turn tail and retreat.

In the east, the news was perhaps worst of all. The Russian dogs refused to die. After the vicious battles of the previous two years, they had licked their wounds and regrouped. Now they were on the march, pushing ever westward. It was as if the Americans and Russians were in a race to reach Berlin. If something did not change soon, the Reich would perish. How had things gone so wrong so quickly?

Karl could not bring himself to care. Just a short while ago, he was a major in the gestapo. He wore his uniform with a fervor that flowed from his very pores. He had done everything he was supposed to: joining the Hitler Youth, graduating from college, and rising through the ranks of the gestapo. All because he believed in the invincibility of the German army and the führer's plan. But ever since that Jewish child and tired, old woman had escaped his grasp, his fervor had turned to bitterness. Peasants had humiliated him. Things had gone inexplicably wrong. If only he could find the brat and the old bat. He would take their throats in his hands and choke the life out of them if it would somehow set everything right again.

He pulled another file off the stack and opened it, glancing down but hardly paying attention. The reports were so boring they made his eyes water, and oftentimes he had to fight the urge to fall asleep. Especially on a day after he had been on one of his off-duty excursions.

Just as he was about to skip to the bottom and give the report its official stamp, a sentence caught his eye. He sat up straight at his desk. *"Informant reports a merchant near the village of Holsta who trades supplies with two men who are believed to be sympathizers. After questioning, the merchant admits the men will bring him scrap metal at night in exchange for milk, flour, and other staples. He has tried to learn their whereabouts with no success. The men trade for far more than they need. Informant suspects large group of* Juden *hiding somewhere nearby."*

A pair of Jews coming out of the shadows to gather large quantities of supplies. It was a lead. The first that Captain Von Duesen had found in months. It might be nothing. But the report came from the same area where his group of *Juden* had first been captured. Perhaps these Jews would know where the boy and the old woman were. He hoped they had not died. He wanted to be the one to kill them.

Von Duesen took the report and stuffed it inside his coat. He had a map of the area in his desk drawer, so he grabbed that, too. And because none of the other officers were paying attention to what he was doing, he stuffed a few extra clips of ammunition for his Luger in his pockets.

He left headquarters and hurried down the street to the motor pool, where he signed out a truck. The sergeant in charge made no notice of his request. Von Duesen fueled it up and headed north.

He would find these Jews, and he would kill them. Or he would die trying.

Before this had happened, he would never have disobeyed orders, would never have taken such rash action. He always did what he was told in support of the führer.

But now, the fate of the führer no longer mattered. All Karl cared about was revenge.

CHAPTER THIRTY-ONE

The Priest's Grotto felt much safer to Anton than the other cave they had hidden in. At least at first. For one thing, it was enormous. The cave's passages went on for many kilometers. The most important feature, though, was the underground lake that kept them fully supplied with water.

His uncle Dmitri explained to him that this cave was composed primarily of gypsum instead of limestone. Both of them were soft minerals, which meant that for thousands of years water had worked its way through the ground to carve out the nooks and crannies they now lived in. The gypsum was soft enough to work with. They carved benches, stools, and even tables from the rock. All in all, it was a good place to be trapped.

But the elders reminded them every day that they

were still in grave danger. The women and children did not leave the cave under any circumstances. Dmitri and the other men would go foraging only when supplies ran low.

The whole community did their best to make life in the cave as normal as possible. Bubbe and the other women did everything they could to keep their traditions alive. They observed the Sabbath, and feasted on whatever they had available. It was tough to keep kosher, but Bubbe promised that God would forgive them.

The days passed slowly. Weeks turned into months, and still they remained hidden. Eventually, Anton went out with Dmitri on supply runs. Bubbe argued against it, of course, but Dmitri convinced her that he and the other men could use an extra pair of hands.

Anton became adept at locating vegetable gardens. They would take just enough to keep the farmers from noticing that any of their crops were missing. He helped gather winter wheat, which the women in the cave ground into flour. But potatoes were his specialty. Anton developed a sixth sense for looting potato fields.

Hanukkah came that winter, and everyone in the cave agreed that his bubbe made the best latkes. It was a good thing, too—often there was nothing else to eat.

Though there were no candles to light or presents to exchange, Anton helped the littlest children make dreidels out of wood. He wished his friend Daniel were there to charm them with his gentle, teasing smiles. Anton did not know where Daniel could be— Dmitri had not seen him since the ambush. Anton hoped that his friend had found another safe place to hide from the Nazis. He refused to believe Daniel had been captured. Every day Anton waited for his friend to appear. Occasionally, newcomers would arrive at the cave and the community would take them in. But none of them ever turned out to be Daniel.

In the spring, they observed Passover. Bubbe had the small ones sweep away the dirt on the cavern floor, while the women washed the dishes and cooked a fine meal. They ate heartily that first evening. On a supply run, Dmitri had even managed to trade for two bottles of wine. They poured a glass for the prophet Elijah, and thanked God for all of the many blessings they were grateful for.

We are still alive, thought Anton. *Whatever else may happen, at least I can be thankful for that.*

It was difficult to find out news of the war. Once, Dmitri managed to bring home a three-month-old French newspaper. No one could read it, but there were pictures of American soldiers in the streets of Paris. This brought cheers and a celebratory dinner for the group that night. The Americans were pushing the Germans back, but the Germans counterattacked. The Russians were moving west, but the Luftwaffe, the German air force, kept them from making any real progress. No one knew what to believe.

One night, while Anton and Dmitri were returning from a foraging trip, a niggling thought itched at the back of Anton's mind. He knew they needed to hurry—they had gone farther from the cave than usual and it would be daylight soon—but he could not seem to ignore it.

"Uncle Dmitri, may I ask you a question?"

"Of course, nephew," Dmitri answered.

"Do you suppose something happened to Daniel?" He paused. "Something bad?"

"No, I do not."

"Why?"

"Because I have faith."

"Why?" Anton repeated.

"You must always trust in God, Anton," his uncle said softly. Dmitri could sense that something was troubling Anton.

"What about Rina and her child? Didn't they have faith?"

"Rina was a devout woman. I am sure she believed that God would watch over her."

"And yet she and her son are dead."

"This is a conversation for a rabbi, which I am not. Faith is belief in things we cannot know or see. Things we are not meant to understand. It is a belief that God has a plan. What happened to Rina and her son was tragic. I cannot explain to you why it happened. But you must pray for them. And for God to guide you—to guide us. I'm sorry, Anton. Sorry for all of this. That we live in a cave like animals. That we must scrounge for food like rats. You should be enjoying your childhood. Of all of us, sometimes I feel it is you who has lost the most. You were so young when your mother died." Dmitri sighed. "As I said, God's plan is God's plan. We do as he commands us. The rest . . . I'm sorry . . . I have no words."

They walked on in silence, but a cacophony of questions pinged around Anton's head. All day long and into the night, he had felt uneasy, as if something was about to happen. He could not rid himself of the feelings.

"Do you think my father is alive?"

He heard his uncle breathe in sharply.

They walked on for a while before Dmitri answered. "I do not know. I am being truthful with you. I truly do not know. But I fear he may not be."

"Why?" Anton felt his chest tighten.

"You were too young to remember. Or perhaps Bubbe kept it from you. Your father enlisted in the Polish cavalry in July 1939. But the Poles did not have tanks like we think of when we hear the word *cavalry* today. Their cavalry was made up of men on horseback. The Germans attacked Poland that September. And the Germans did have tanks. And artillery and an infantry. The Germans' assault was swift and vicious. They called the style *blitzkrieg*. It means 'lightning war.' The Polish army was nearly destroyed. Those who were not captured were killed. So I do not know what has become of your father. If he survived, he could still be alive. Perhaps he is a prisoner of war. But if I know my brother, he would not cower or run away from a fight no matter the odds. If ever there were a man who would take on a Panzer tank with nothing more than a horse and a sword, it would be my brother Nikolai. I wish I could give you an answer. All we can hope for is to learn his fate once this terrible war has ended. I'm sorry. I know it is not what you wished to hear. Now we must hurry. Light is coming and we must be in the cave before the sun comes up. There are German troops still about."

On they walked through the woods, the light growing brighter in the east. As they crept closer to the cave's entrance, the uneasy feeling Anton had not been able to shake grew stronger.

Suddenly, Anton heard shouting in the distance. The screams of his friends—no, his family—filled his ears. Sergei Serniov. Eva Birnbaum. Little Lena Weiss. Anton and Dmitri dropped their sacks of food and ran.

Something was very wrong. Their people always whispered. They would only be shouting if they had been ambushed. Then came the sound Anton prayed he wouldn't hear. His bubbe's voice.

And this time, Anton did not know how he would protect her.

CHAPTER
THIRTY-TWO

In the end, it had been easy. The *Juden* thought they were so clever. Karl was surprised no one had thought of it before. The intelligence report had led him to a small village to the north. He had interrogated the informant who knew which of the town's residents was trading with the *Juden*. Maksym Shevchenko. It had not taken much to find out where this man lived, and drive the short distance to his house. No matter that it was the wee hours of the morning. No matter that he had been demoted. He was still a captain of the gestapo, which Shevchenko would do well to respect.

As soon as the peasant walked out onto the porch, Von Duesen could sense his fear. Shevchenko wore a straw hat, which he removed and worked nervously in his hands. His wife followed him, and though Shevchenko tried to order her back inside, she refused and clutched his arm.

"*Guten Tag, Herr* Shevchenko," Von Duesen called out. *Good day.* He would not do them the courtesy of speaking Ukrainian. The man and his wife nodded, but did not reply.

"I am looking for two men. I understand you trade with them."

"*Nein.*" The man shook his head.

"Are you certain? I have this information on very good authority."

"*Nein, mein* captain," the man said. "I know of no such men."

Von Duesen sighed. It was nearly dawn. Inside the house he could see the warm glow from a lantern. He had probably interrupted their breakfast.

"Are you certain, *Herr* Shevchenko?" he asked again.

"*Ja,*" the man said.

Von Duesen pulled the Luger from his belt. He pointed it at Shevchenko's wife and shot her in the thigh. She fell to the ground, her screams so high-pitched and agonizing that it was actually painful to Von Duesen's ears. Shevchenko dropped to his knees, his hands pressing on her thigh to try and stop the bleeding. He cursed the captain as the woman continued her keening wail. The noise was giving Von Duesen a headache.

"Tell her to be quiet or I will shoot her again," he said calmly.

The man sobbed as he spoke quietly to his wife, who tried valiantly to silence herself.

"Now. The men—where do they come from? They want for supplies for more than two people. Where are they hiding?"

"*Mein* captain," the man pleaded. "I do not know. Please. Please!"

Von Duesen shot the wife in the right elbow. She screamed again, and to Von Duesen's relief she passed out, her blood pouring out of her and staining the porch. Shevchenko begged Von Duesen for mercy.

"If you do not tell me what I want to know, the next shot will be between her eyes."

Shevchenko was breathing so heavily he could barely speak. "No. No, please. Please, *mein* captain! I will tell you what I know. I have heard rumors only. The men, they bring scrap metal, which I can sell. They say nothing about where they come from or where they find the scrap. We trade and then they leave."

Von Duesen raised the Luger, pointing it at the woman's face.

"Say your good-byes. I will kill your wife, but I will leave you alive, to mourn, and to remind you how stupid you are. Your wife will die because you chose to protect a group of Jewish dogs instead of her."

"No, *mein* captain," Shevchenko pleaded. He put himself between the gun and his wife. "I do not know for certain! As I said, I have heard rumors. There is a place called the Priest's Grotto. It is not far from here. It is a large cave. I have heard that the Jews hide there. Only the men come out and only at night."

Von Duesen lowered the Luger to his side and returned it to his holster. He pulled the map from inside his uniform jacket and spread it open on the hood of his truck.

"Show me where it is."

From there, it had been so simple. Von Duesen had gone to the Priest's Grotto. And he had found exactly whom he was looking for.

THIRTY-THREE

"Anton," Dmitri whispered. "We must slow down. We don't know what is happening. If it is the gestapo, we must be careful."

Anton knew Dmitri was right, but he had a horrible feeling their hiding place had been discovered. Images of Rina and David gunned down like animals flew through his mind. He could not calm himself. His uncle finally grabbed him by the shoulder and jerked him to a stop.

"Anton," Dmitri said harshly. "Listen to me! We must be quiet. If the gestapo has found the cave, we will need to make sure we are not seen."

Anton was finally able to calm himself. He knew his uncle was right. Anton and Dmitri crept out of the forest quietly, but kept themselves hidden in the underbrush. The sun was clearing the eastern horizon. In the morning light they could see all the residents of the cave standing just outside its entrance. And there in front of them, Bubbe trembled on her knees. And a familiar face hovered behind hers—the young gestapo officer who had already taken her prisoner once.

He held his pistol at her temple. Her eyebrow was cut and bleeding. He must have knocked her to the ground. And now the look on his face said that was only the beginning. Herman and Sergei tried to intervene, but the German forced them back by pointing his gun.

"Bubbe!" Anton cried. He burst from the underbrush and ran toward his grandmother.

"No, Anton!" he heard Dmitri and Bubbe shout at the same time. Their voices sounded low and far away against the thumping sound of Anton's heart beating in his ears.

Recognition burned in the Nazi's eyes.

"You!" he shouted. "At last I have found you, you little Jewish pig! Now you die!" He swung the pistol around and took aim at Anton just as Bubbe leapt from the ground. She threw herself between Anton and her tormentor as he pulled the trigger. The explosion sounded like a thunderclap. The bullet ripped into her torso and she fell forward on the man who had shot her. He struggled to shove the old woman's body aside, and when he finally succeeded, he took aim at Anton once again.

There were ten meters between them. Anton ran toward the officer as fast as he could. At the last second, he closed his eyes, certain he was about to die. And in that moment, he began to pray. If this was God's plan, as his uncle Dmitri had told him, so be it. Without Bubbe, he had nothing. His only chance was to get to the German before he got a shot off. He would kill the man with his bare hands.

He realized he was too late the instant he heard the *boom* of a single gunshot. Anton waited for the bullet to rend his flesh. But nothing happened. He felt no pain. Perhaps this is how one died. When he opened his eyes, he could not fathom what he was seeing. The officer's body lay next to Bubbe on the ground. He had been shot through the head.

But Anton's grandmother was still breathing. He ran to her side and dropped to his knees. "Bubbe! Bubbe!" he shouted, taking her by the shoulders. "Someone help her!" he pleaded to his friends and neighbors. They looked at him, then looked away. He felt Uncle Dmitri's hand on his shoulder. Bubbe had been shot in the stomach. Blood soaked her dress. In spite of this, she opened her eyes and smiled at him. She reached her gnarled hand up and touched his cheek.

"Anton, my good boy," she whispered. "Someday, you will understand this love . . ." Her words were interrupted by a horrible, wracking cough. "It is all I have to give you. My love." She closed her eyes and was gone.

Tears flowed down Anton's cheeks. He could not stop them. He did not want to stop them. And he did not understand what had just happened. Bubbe had saved him. The gestapo officer was dead. But how?

He looked up to see Uncle Dmitri standing over him, his eyes also filled with tears. All of the families that had come to know Bubbe cried along with them.

Then an unfamiliar noise caught Anton's attention. At the edge of the tree line stood a group of armed men. Pavel was among them and held a still-smoking rifle. He had reunited with his militia.

Anton recognized another face. Daniel. He held a shotgun, but did not quite look at home among the militia members. How good it was to see his old friend's face!

Uncle Pavel came toward them, and Anton could see that his eyes were ringed with redness. "The Germans are on the run," Pavel told them. "The Russian army is less than five kilometers to the west. We . . . all . . . we are safe, now. I only wish we could have gotten here sooner," he said, before bowing his head in prayer.

Anton looked at his bubbe, whom he still held in his arms. Then he stared long and hard at the body of a man so full of evil he had made an old woman his nemesis. Now the Nazi was nothing more than an empty shell. His lifeless eyes stared up at the sky like a doll's.

"Safety is an illusion," Anton said. "We will never be safe. Not while men like this walk the earth."

Anton gently laid his bubbe on the ground, and then he prayed through his tears.

EPILOGUE

Daniel came to live on the family farm with Anton and Dmitri. He had nowhere—and no one—to return to, and Anton was happy to have the company. Uncle Pavel had chosen to rejoin the militia and chase the Nazis out of Ukraine.

The Germans were sure to lose. Men and women of good conscience would defeat evil. Every day, Anton thought about what the war had stolen from him. His childhood. His bubbe. His father. Uncle Dmitri did his best to keep his nephew's spirits up. Anton and Daniel helped him work the farm, and even found occasional time to read and explore. But nothing felt the same anymore.

One morning, Anton woke up with a decision made. He packed his blanket with a map, a canteen, some matches, and some bread and potatoes he'd nabbed from the kitchen the night before. He tried to be quiet, but failed—he and Daniel shared the room and his friend was a light sleeper.

"Are you going somewhere?" Daniel asked with a yawn.

"Yes," Anton answered. "West. To Poland. I'm going to find my father."

"Anton, what if your father is . . ."

"Then at least I will know."

"Have you told Dmitri?"

"No. He will forbid me to go."

"What should I tell him?"

"You won't have to. He will know why I must go."

"Are you sure this is the right thing to do? There is still a war out there."

"There is always a war."

Daniel had nothing to say to that.

"Thank you for letting me stay here, Anton," Daniel said. "I hope you and your father will come home one day soon. I would like to meet him."

Anton shook Daniel's hand and quietly crept through the house. He left through the kitchen door, and as he stepped outside, he took one last look around the farm in the gathering light.

Then he pulled up his collar around his neck and headed west into the cool, fine morning.

Though *The Enemy Above* is fiction, it is based on real events. The Priest's Grotto still exists, and while it no longer harbors Jewish refugees, it serves as a stark reminder of the horror that all Jews faced during World War II. Several Jewish families used it as a safe haven during the Nazi occupation of Western Ukraine. This area is filled with limestone and gypsum caves, and many refugees took advantage of the terrain to escape Adolf Hitler's *Judenfrei* policy.

When I began working on this book, I quickly discovered the near impossibility of finding words to describe the enormity of the horror and death during the Holocaust. Millions of Jews, Poles, Ukrainians, and people from other ethnic groups were exterminated by a madman—one it took the combined might of the world's greatest nations to defeat. The magnitude of the loss of so much human potential makes words seem empty and meaningless.

But as Bubbe says in *The Enemy Above*, Jews were persecuted for centuries before Hitler came to power. After the Russian Revolution, attacks on Jewish settlements, called *pogroms,* killed and destroyed the property of hundreds of thousands of Jews. And in this area of Western Ukraine, Jewish families were under constant assault for hundreds of years. In fact, many Jews throughout Europe were slow to believe that Hitler's threat was out of the ordinary. Many saw it as just another in a long line of assaults against their very existence. By the time they discovered the magnitude of Hitler's plans, it was already too late for millions of people.

Yet somehow in the midst of this suffering, the tenacity of the human spirit took root. When tyranny and oppression are opposed, they can ultimately be defeated. It may take years, decades, even centuries, but in the end the human desire for freedom and self-determination can win out. The fight for survival can be more powerful than any weapon or ideology.

In researching this novel, I found that the story of those who hid in the Priest's Grotto was not unique.

Many of the people whom Adolf Hitler considered inferior survived by their wits and ingenuity. They hid in caves, deep within forests, or high in mountain ranges. Some, like the Bielski brothers, took up arms and retreated deep into the forests of German-occupied Poland. Their guerilla warfare against the Nazis saved the lives of thousands of Jews. Men like Oskar Schindler risked their lives to smuggle hundreds of Jews to freedom. Undoubtedly, there are many more undiscovered stories of those who found the ability to survive amid a horrible tragedy.

I hope someday their stories are told.

SOURCES

Berkhoff, Karel C. *Harvest of Despair: Life and Death in Ukraine Under Nazi Rule*. Cambridge: Belknap Press, 2008.

Macgosci, Paul Robert. *A History of Ukraine*. Toronto: University of Toronto Press, 1995.

NationalGeographic.com

Nicola, Christos and Peter Lane Taylor. *The Secret of Priest's Grotto: A Holocaust Survival Story*. Minneapolis: Kar-Ben Publishing, 2007.

ACKNOWLEDGMENTS

I owe a great deal of thanks to so many people for helping me to shape this book. First off, I need to thank my editor, Jenne Abramowitz, for molding the story into shape. Every writer should be so lucky to have such an editor. I also owe a debt of gratitude to Jana Haussmann at Scholastic Book Fairs for encouraging me to pursue this novel. In fact, I'm just going to go all in and say a great big thank-you to everyone at Scholastic for being such a great publisher and helping me grow as a writer.

My family, as always, is my source of strength and inspiration. In particular, my wife, Kelly, deserves far more praise for her help and encouragement than I could ever confine to the pages of this book. My children, Mick, Jessica, and Rachel, do nothing except provide me with laughter and joy every single day. I love you all.

ABOUT THE AUTHOR

Michael P. Spradlin is a *New York Times* bestselling author. His books include *Into the Killing Seas*, the Youngest Templar trilogy, the Wrangler Award winner *Off Like the Wind!: The First Ride of the Pony Express*, the Killer Species series, and several other novels and picture books. He holds a black belt in television remote control and is fluent in British, Canadian, Australian, and several other English-based languages. He lives in Lapeer, Michigan.

Visit him online at www.michaelspradlin.com.